I See

France

CeCe DeLuc

Illustrated by Betc McNamara

Copyright © 2019 CeCe deLuc

All rights reserved.

ISBN: 978-1-7341329-0-8

DEDICATION

I'm sure you'll agree that to be a
writer, you must also be a reader. Of all
of the things, my mother gave us the
love of reading was the one that rubbed
off on me the most. Oh, sure patience,
generosity, integrity – I got all
that <u>and</u> her lasagna recipe. But
reading...that formed me. We
read *everything*, and then, one year we
subscribed to Harlequin Romances and
my future was set. Mom saw the
dreamer in me and faced me in that
direction.

I also dedicate this book to my aunt,
Nancy McNamara, who brought
France to me and me to France. It
was *that* trip with Nancy and her
friends that inspired this book and my
crush on Paris.

ACKNOWLEDGMENTS

I've had a lot of help over the years, but perhaps the help that goes the farthest back was from my 8th Grade social studies teacher, Ms. Patricia Cote, who took the time to tutor me on adjectives and adverbs after school. She was an excellent, hard-working, and kind, teacher. Thank you.

I also have some friends who have encouraged me and made a difference in my determination to publish. Aunt Beth, Brenda, April, Deanne, Cris, Mary, and Ann, thank you.

And who can live without their sisters? Amy and Betc have read, re-read, edited, and drawn for me. I hope I've given them as much.

PREQUEL

❝ You know Ellen, there are aspects of your personality that are really annoying," Eric said

"And let's face it – you and I are only dating because we worked together. You were an easy – um – date. Always alone, never terribly popular in the group. I don't know if it's your ridiculous, sophomoric obsession with France. But, let's face it – you are a 30-year-old woman with the daydreams of a 13-year-old. The world isn't like that – this isn't a romance novel. This is day-to-day survival, and you need a harder edge. I am not Prince Charming, and so you can stop waiting for me to pop the question, I'm not going to.

I've had to think about my future, and I know that I have a different vision of the woman I will marry, and she is the polar opposite of you. She is a beautiful blond, tall and lanky – not a short, plump redhead. She is a professional woman who can handle a job, and family and is not waiting for someone to come along and marry her. She has self-respect, not an unhealthy attachment with a romanticized version of the world. She is a reader of non-fiction and a woman with multiple degrees. Our children will attain their success from achievement not from daydreaming. I'm very sorry, but you're not going to be my wife or my lover anymore. Not that you were much of a lover."

"Ok. Eric are you finished? Feel better? I'm sorry you have been operating under the delusion that we'd marry – that you'd put that much thought into it but let me relieve your mind right now." I paused for a breath. Even knowing how Eric was, I was surprised by his rant. And now, I would take an opportunity to straighten him out.

"I can't imagine what a life, married to you would be like. I know that I wouldn't be able to trust you; you'd treat me like a piece of property and not a person. That you'd favor a night spent ogling strippers to a night spent reading. That you'd always smell of dirty socks and have something stuck in your teeth.

I'm not sure how you will attract that tall, lanky blond because you seem to forget what YOU look like. You're overweight for a man 3 inches taller than you, your hairline is beginning to creep away, and you spit a little when you try to make a point."

With that, Ellen got out of Eric's 1999 Toyota Corolla and caught a bus. On the way home, she wondered why she'd stayed with Eric after that first date. *Am I really that girl that thinks Better a bad boyfriend than none at all?* she thought.

Prequel

10 YEARS EARLIER

"Merde!"

At five past midnight on the 17th of May, Charles stood in the courtyard of the Louvre – dwarfed by the illuminated I. M. Pei pyramids, while around him an army of police scurried back and forth. Charles could still hear the alarm pealing, even though it had been silenced 15 minutes earlier.

And now, one less painting hung on the walls of the Louvre. One, ironically, that had been donated by Charles' own family. And sadly, now, *stolen* by one of Charles' own family.

Charles Blanchard had been right – it had been tonight, and it had been taken. And there was nothing he could do about it because the museum didn't believe him when he warned them, and his superiors, anxious to curry favor with the board of the museum, hadn't supported him.

And Charles was devastated because he'd tried to prevent it.

Marco had taunted him with clues. There was the photograph of the painting that had now been stolen - the envelope had a return address of 'Louvre Museum'; a note found in Charles' mailbox referred to Charles' father's untimely death on the 16th of May, and finally, the newspaper article found taped to his door one evening, which mentioned a family's legacy lost.

Charles and Marco had been raised like brothers until Charles' father died and Marco felt his place as a Blanchard was at risk. Marco had been orphaned twice – once when his own parents (Charles' paternal aunt and her husband) died and once when Charles Sr. (Charles' father) died. Now that boy Charles had grown up with was a well-known thief.

Charles knew that he was the only one now who could restore the painting – but Marco'd had time to plan and time to escape. Finding him now could take years.

CHAPTER 1

"Bonjour! Emile -- just the usual!"

I watched as Emile bagged up an authentic French croissant and a large French Roast Coffee, took my exact change and opened the door for me. The only thing better than this service would be ordering that breakfast from a sidewalk café on the Boulevard St. Germain.

The "usual" for me always carried that French 'accent'. My small dog - Gigi, my favorite wine - Beaujolais, the ringtone on my phone -- *La Vie en Rose*! So, it was no surprise that I started every day as a Frenchwoman might.

I had been enthralled by France in general, and Paris in particular for as long as I could remember. This morning as I collected my breakfast and paper and boarded the T to work, I could imagine myself jamming into the Paris Metro.

I settled into a seat opposite an older man and a young punker and chose to withdraw into the paper. I spent several minutes scanning the front page and then turned to the inside pages. My eyes drifted up and down until something caught my attention -- *'French Police renew investigation into missing Hassam work.'* The story went on to explain about the Childe Hassam painting - *'Quai du Louvre'* (a sentimental favorite of mine) stolen nearly ten years earlier from the Louvre and never recovered. As it was nearing the tenth anniversary, the Louvre and the French authorities were revisiting the circumstances of the crime and had posted photographs of the missing artwork. I allowed myself to linger a bit and daydream about a someday trip to Paris. *I'd love to see the Louvre, cruise on the Seine and dance with a handsome Frenchman on the banks of the river.*

My dreaming was short-circuited by a sense of movement around me, and the notion that I'd heard my stop called. Gathering my things, I joined the queue to leave and start a new day in the rainy chill of a Boston autumn.

A few weeks later, after the utter humiliation of having to box up my office and ship it to another state, it sank in. I was officially unemployed. I had been laid off, as were the majority of the people I worked with. Our competitor had bought us and permanently closed the local office.

Eleven years of my life had been spent there and, yet my company had pretty much told me that they didn't want me anymore -- like almost every one of the 3 serious boyfriends I'd had.

So, no boyfriend, no job. Except for my family and friends, I had no attachments and seemingly nothing I could count as special.

The upside was, my company had paid me to go away and despite the shocking loss of my sense of self -- I had a lot of money! It wasn't until later that I realized it was a life-changing amount of money.

Over the next few weeks, I sent out a million resumes and received many responses indicating I was rather far down the list of applicants for that particular job. The chances of me hearing from them again, slim. But, one of my most under-recognized personality traits is my tenacity and, so, I just kept looking and applying until I found… Mr. Douglas, my new employer.

Gavin Douglas was CPA and no more boring a man ever existed. He was balding, married, with (I'm sure) 2.4 children and brought a tuna fish sandwich to work every day. He never raised his voice and never was animated about anything. His business was domestic only, and even his clients were nearly Quaker-like in nature. It was a pleasant place to work- just. Not exciting, not thrilling. But, he liked me enough to hire me, I was surprisingly well paid and for the time being, settled.

Until Saturday afternoon. Christmas Eve! Turns out that Santa is thinking about us big kids too!

On Christmas Eve, I pulled into my parents' driveway, pleased to see that my aunt Cathy's car was already there. Cathy was Dad's sister, and I adored her! We'd taken vacations together in the past but after my grandmother died, Aunt Cathy, who'd been her caregiver because she'd never married, had moved away. Now, Cathy lived a few hours away near another of my aunts, and I rarely saw her. Fortunately, she was here for Christmas.

"Aunt Cathy! I've missed you!" I cried out as I entered the house.

"What are we, chopped liver?" Dad asked with a drawl. Dad was always willing to tease, and he could take it too. As a matter of fact, he was often the butt of jokes through our growing up years.

Mom herself was a great, good sport playing off Dad and also ending up the butt of jokes herself.

"Come here honey and tell me about that new job!" Aunt Cathy said, expecting an exciting story.

"I wish I could tell you I'd found out that Mr. Douglas was a spy or a crook - but no luck there — he is just about the most boring person on God's Green Earth," I explained with a bit of a whine.

Cathy who might have worked for the 2nd most boring person on the planet in her prior life laughed at my expression and offered her take on the situation … "Darling, that is job security. Get your excitement elsewhere — for instance, how about coming to Paris and London with me in April?"

"I know what — — wait a minute — Paris in the Spring?" I exclaimed. "April in Paris?" I was practically having palpitations.

It was serendipity really -- I had a pile of cash burning a hole in my pocket after being laid off, and my Aunt wanted me to go to Paris and London with her.

Before she finished her sentence, I responded with a hearty "Oui!"

As a voracious reader of romantic fiction, where the girl went to France on holiday, I imagined meeting some impoverished or deposed duke or, even better, a prince; having the whirlwind romance of my life culminating with me going home with him to be introduced to the remaining kin.

Of course, there was always some dark secret; another woman or some intrigue involved; but, I figured, I was only going to Paris for four days, then onto London, so how much intrigue could there be time for?

Ok so maybe Eric was right -- I was a romantic.

This is what I needed! I needed to get away and where better than Paris?

"Put me down for it — I have been dying to go to Paris - When do we leave?" My mind was racing — *would boring Mr. Douglas give me the time off?*

"Yes, and London! Doesn't it sound wonderful?" Cathy said with less excitement than I was showing.

"Oh - how long will we be there?" A key question.

"We leave April 15th and return on the 23rd - 8 days." my Aunt explained factually.

"So, 4 months from now. Merry Christmas to me! I exclaimed.

And, that was the day my life was changed. What had moments before been a gray life — with no peaks (or valleys) was now bathed in a rosy glow.

Fast forward to April 15th;

"Come on, Ellen, let's get the bags in the hallway, Nora will be here in a few minutes to take us to the airport."

Boring Mr. Douglas had enthusiastically given me the time off — seems he had a liaison during WWII in Paris. Shocking, I know!

I had never left the United States. I would be traveling with a group of older women — Aunt Cathy's friends — mainly teachers and such, all well-traveled, so I was sure I'd be safe.

I'd get to see all the things I'd only thought about - where Monet painted and lived; I'd climb the Eiffel Tower and wander the Louvre; I'd see the White Cliffs of Dover.

My aunt Cathy would be my partner on this trip --and if her friends were as fun to be around as Aunt Cathy, I was in luck.

Cathy and I had always had a close relationship. She was my father's eldest sister, but like many Irish first daughters, she never married and therefore got to have her own adventures. Cathy'd traveled widely but secretly told me that coming back home was her favorite destination. And, although she was considerably older than I was, Cathy and I had a blast together. I don't think she ever thought about her age unless she was sitting in her hairdresser's chair. She had a strawberry blonde halo of hair encircling a porcelain oval face. Her eyes, like her birthstone, Aquamarine. Though she was over 70 now, her figure was trim and her face and hands unlined. Cathy has grown up in the 30s and early forties and was always turned out like a bandbox. She was distinguished without pretension.

I only took after her a bit; we shared a sense of humor, I suppose. Instead, I am as likely to have run a stocking or dripped toothpaste on myself, as Cathy was to have found just the right dress for every occasion!

So, I stood there, bags in hand, planning my wardrobe for the moment we touched down in Paris — as if Monsieur Droite (Mr. Right) would be waiting at the baggage carousel at Orly for me.

First, I had to get to the airport.

Herding our luggage out to the car, it became very obvious to me, which one of us was better prepared -- Cathy being a seasoned traveler had just one bag. I had the largest most awkward suitcase available, a cosmetics case and a tote bag containing water, snacks including chocolate and two books which I imagined I would need on such a long flight.

"Ellen, can't you fit your cosmetics in the suitcase? You're going to regret having to drag that bag from plane to taxi and, you'll be exhausted before you even get to Paris." Cathy pointed out.

Cathy clearly knew what she was talking about, but so did I! She apparently didn't realize that this was the same girl who took an evening dress on her trip to Florida several years before! Bad example though – the hotel we stayed in on that trip was a MOtel, not a HOtel and the most dressed up we got was a nice pair of shorts and a silk tank top for dinner at one of the restaurants on the strip in Orlando.

Mom had been so sweet to make that gorgeous (polyester double-knit) gown for my trip – but it would have been kinder if she had told me that there weren't many 'evening gown' occasions for an 18-year-old girl at Disney. Even now, I'm blushing at my rank naïveté.

However, as a rookie at international travel, I insisted I needed to have a separate cosmetics case - just like I imagined everyone dressed for flight! Out of the corner of my eye, something caught my attention - my 70-year-old aunt lifting my suitcase into the back of the SUV!

"Wait! Aunt Cathy, you can't lift that – I'll put it in the trunk!" I pulled the door closed behind me and ran to the car. After gently taking the suitcase from my Aunt I put it in the trunk and apologized for my day-dreaming.

CHAPTER 2

T he rest of the day we moved from one mode of transport to another. The car to the airport; the small plane to Newark; and finally, at 7:45pm, we were uncomfortably installed on the aircraft that we were sentenced to for the next six hours - the flight that would take me to Paris!

I say 'sentenced to' because the plane was absolutely full. I didn't see one empty seat. I suppose it could have been a comfort to those with a fear of flying. How could anyone get hurt in an airplane accident with so many people keeping them hemmed in? Just trying to get out to the aisle to go to the restroom, involved people in the front row holding their breath, while the rest of the passengers (who did that before they left home) shed unnecessary layers of clothing.

Finally, sitting on the plane and listening, I was preparing for my foray into France. It seemed that easily two-thirds of the plane was occupied by expatriate or vacationing Parisiennes. Listening to this chatter, it all sounded so perfect and so coincidental (what are the chances that a flight to Paris would have French people on it?). I was listening to the voices around me with rose-colored ears. I was sure they were discussing the latest Chanel collection; debating world politics or even planning a coup; when in fact, they were probably talking about the same things we were, the movie; the possibility of a riot if one got up to go to the restroom; where they parked the car before they left.

Eating dinner required a tag-team approach. I would eat, and my aunt would sit quietly with her arms straight up in the air (to allow me elbow room). After I polished off my Beef Teriyaki, Rice Pilaf, and Green Peas and downed the last of my Chocolate Cake, I signaled to the steward to take my tray away and bring my aunt hers. I would then sit quietly with my arms in the air (actually helps the digestion, come to find out) until Cathy finished her dinner. She, of course already had my review of the meal, so the palate was prepared.

I had done some flying in my life – to Florida a few times for vacation and to DC as well, and then there was that long period of weekly flights to Philly, but every time it was a short flight. This flight was seven hours – nearly a workday!

Even the airline seemed to acknowledge that it was going to be a long flight, because, a few hours into the trip the lights dimmed and on the movie screen at the front of the cabin was displayed a map of just where in the world we were. There was a little plane that was tracking our progress across the "pond." I say pond because I was trying to ignore the fact that flying over the Atlantic Ocean was sort of freaking me out! I am all about the end result – once I got over the ocean I'd be in Europe, but it seemed to me that if something happened to the plane over the Atlantic, it would majorly cut into my time in Paris!

"Ellen, you seem kind of anxious," Aunt Cathy said, apparently tipped off by my fixation on the never-moving-lighted dot. My hands gripped the arms of my seat, and my mouth was set in a tight line.

"Why don't we have a glass of wine to celebrate our trip! – Stewardess, two glasses of Red Wine, please." Cathy then turned her attention back to me. "Remember, we're going to Paris – doesn't matter how we get there. Let's talk about what you want to see."

As we chatted and sipped our Beaujolais, I tried to sit more comfortably in my tiny seat, and gradually, the talk of people watching in little café's and seeing the *Winged Victory of Samothrace* began to relax me. After 10 or 15 minutes, I realized that the dot had moved, and my hands were calmly folded in my lap. Cathy, realizing I was not going to flip out on the plane, changed the subject and we debated what the movie would be.

The movie turned out to be *A Good Year*. Suitably French in subject matter, and I dozed pleasantly through it. My aunt, however, was spending her time trying to get comfortable. As stoic as she was, there was definitely no extra room to stretch out, and her face and throat were glazed with perspiration by early morning.

Now, waking up in foreign airspace, preparing to disembark an airplane and set foot on really chic soil makes you consider your appearance. I considered it and realized that the fear of looking rumpled and generally grubby was nothing in comparison to the reaction I'd get from my seatmates if I tried to move or get my purse and makeup essentials out of their nesting place between my feet.

Even if I took such a risk, there was no time or space for a makeover.

I tried, God knows, by slipping down in my seat and pulling my bag toward me, but my cosmetics were in the previously maligned cosmetic case, so all I could manage was my tiny hairbrush and a compact. I'd dropped my lipstick – La Vie en Rose Pink, (chosen especially for the trip) and it had rolled under the seat ahead of us. So, I bit my lips and licked them several times to get some color into them. Not the perfect solution, considering my advanced state of dehydration.

Onward! The ugly American had arrived, and she was packing luggage.

CHAPTER 3

After trekking through customs and scoping out the baggage carousel from behind a rather rotund woman (in case there was a member of the duchy waiting for me), we met our guide (Serge) and were hustled onto a small bus for the trip into Paris.

On the bus, I settled into my seat and got out my camera. I took a photo of a highway sign on the way, but really, besides the little cars, there wasn't much to look at on the ride in. I was tired but too excited to sleep, so I decided to check out the women who would be my traveling companions for the next eight days.

Cathy, whom I have already mentioned, is my darling aunt who, although never married, is still very attractive for a woman in her 70s, and more fun than some of my friends.

Cathy is well-read and well-traveled. Happily, she knows how to laugh at stupid jokes and otherwise have a good time.

Jessica is one of the organizers of the trip and also a very distinguished woman. A former school principal, she is now retired and spends much of her time traveling or planning her next trip. She is the mother duckling on this trip.

Susan is co-organizer of the trip and Jessica's best friend. She also is retired from teaching, and I know that between Susan, and Jessica I will get my money's worth from this vacation. Susan is very pragmatic and plain-spoken, has a great sense of humor and loves to travel.

Eleanor is a lovely woman who appears to be in her early to mid-seventies. She seems energetic and enthusiastic about the trip, has been everywhere, and I look forward to making friends with her. Eleanor seems to enjoy everything with enthusiasm and a wry sense of humor.

Laura is also a charming woman seeming to be in her late fifties, possibly early sixties and very much a lady. She reminds me of a preacher's wife, but it turns out she's a docent at a local museum. She is a ditherer, but sweet.

Pauline is Susan's sister and entirely different in every way. Very sophisticated and polished. She was an art history teacher, and I'll depend on her to direct me to the best art. She dresses like a millionairess and sitting here I'm wondering if I could wear a cashmere shawl like Pauline and pull it off.

Vivian is the character on this trip. I've spent under 16 hours with her, and already I realize that. She has an air of an absent-minded professor, with a brochure always in her face, but has the facts at hand when called upon. She is also high maintenance and would need some watching. I have been detailed to keep an eye on her since the only time she didn't wander off was on the plane.

As I continued to observe my companions, I couldn't help but wonder how this trip would go. I remember my first concern when I thought about the trip was how I would get along traveling with 7 older women. Many girls my age would undertake a journey like this with friends their own age, or with husbands or boyfriends. But my friends were marrying, and I had no significant other keeping me home. Traveling with this crowd would guarantee early to bed, but if that was how I was getting to Paris, so be it.

The landscape was starting to change, the light rain that had been falling since we landed at Orly was stopping, and I got my first look at 'downtown Paris.' A thrill ran through me even though it was early in the morning. We were winding through streets bustling with activity.

Serge kindly pointed out the landmarks as we passed them and it seemed that as soon as he said "Viola, la Louvre," he was saying "'ere is your hotel, ladies. I hope you are comfortable."

As a matter of fact, we were across the street from the Tuileries Gardens, which border the Louvre. Within walking distance to the most famous museum in the world! How lucky can a girl get?

I was exhausted, and so was Cathy. I know she looked forward to a nap and a clean face. The flight really wiped both of us out, but I was afraid that the day would slip by and we wouldn't get to do "Paris stuff." After a brief nap, we met up with our traveling companions and set out for the Musee' d'Orsay.

CHAPTER 4

The Musee' d'Orsay sits on the River Seine's left bank, on the other side of the Tuileries Gardens. An old train station, it now houses the most impressive exhibition of impressionist masterpieces that I could ever have imagined. I was thrilled to see several excellent Monet's, but, oddly, the painting that took my breath away was *"Whistler's Mother."* Not the *Mona Lisa*, not a Renoir or a Gauguin, but *"Whistler's Mother."*

I can't explain it except to say that for a "country girl" to be faced with one of the most famous masterpieces in the world was exciting enough, and the painting I had heard about all my life was even more awesome face to face. It was much larger than I had ever expected, and its beauty was its simplicity.

It was when I backed away from the painting that I knocked into this very nondescript looking man who told me that this was a picture of his great-grandmother. ok....

After moving far away from the Parisian nut-ball, I wandered around looking at the other paintings in the area and was stunned to see the wall-sized murals by Toulouse Lautrec. These paintings never figured highly in my limited artistic education, but I liked them. In my opinion, they are like France on canvas. They're a bit faded but nevertheless have a distinctive flavor far removed from Monet, Gauguin or the others.

As I was taking them in, I couldn't help but think about what that funny man had said. Related to Whistler's Mother? Really? I suppose next he'll be telling me that he was the love child of Mary Cassatt and Claude Monet! But there he was again, passing in front of me and I couldn't help but be interested in this unique character.

Perhaps he was one of the disaffected duchies, I had been waiting to meet. I looked him over and wasn't terribly impressed with his appearance. He was a perfectly ordinary looking Frenchmen, in his late 30's with thick, well-combed hair and a good build. He looked as if he was acquainted with the concept of daily hygiene and he certainly dressed neatly -- the polar opposite of the eccentrics you'd see on the T back in Boston -- he wasn't wearing his mother's overcoat or a knit cap with lint balls and other stuff hanging off of it. He wasn't wearing gloves, but I could tell that if he did, they would have fabric all the way over the fingers, not stopping just above the first knuckle. In addition to that I was pretty sure he was talking to me, not one of his resident personalities and surprisingly I wasn't wary of him.

I tried to find my Aunt to see if she had noticed this man, but she was wandering around with Eleanor and seemed to be deeply involved in the exhibit.

As I stood in front of yet another Monet, I found the man beside me again.

"Hello," I spoke quietly to him, "God, you just can't see too many Monet's, can you? My name is Ellen, and yours is?"

"Charles," my new friend said softly."

"Would that be Charles Whistler?" I queried. I know it sounded slightly sarcastic, but I couldn't resist. Strangely, I was fascinated with this guy and instantly felt comfortable with him. Typically, though, I reserve my caustic wit for people who know me well and will still like me in the morning. I was really taking a chance. Who knew? I could piss this guy off, and he'd end up throwing me off the Pont Neuf into the chilly Seine. I looked over at him to see if I'd sent him foaming at the mouth and at that very moment, he answered me.

"Actually, - I'm not related to Whistler, but this painting always has struck me as having a story behind it. One of my favorite pastimes, when I visit is to imagine what had been going on to cause his mother to look so grim! My last name is Blanchard," he said in his best flat-toned English accent.

"And what have you imagined set Mrs. Whistler off today?" I asked him with a mixture of caustic humor and sincere curiosity.

"Well, what I believe happened is that the painter, James did something that caused a ruckus – perhaps he let out the chickens when he fed them – or perhaps he was a poor student who brought home a failing mark on a report card – believe me I've seen that look before! And what I believe happened here is that he wanted to mollify his mother and to show her what he was good at, so he sat her down in her worn chair and painted her at that very moment!"

I chuckled and realized that he had immediately set my mind at ease.

"I'm sorry about that crack about your last name, but you just took me by surprise. And, I momentarily believed that you either were related or were maybe a little – eccentric." My name is Ellen Devlin," I continued to babble, giving this gentleman (and he indeed was a gentleman) ample reason to back away and find a new friend, but he just stood there nodding his head.

"Would you like to have a cup of cafe au lait? They have an excellent restaurant here." Charles asked politely. He seemed perfectly reasonable to me now, but I wasn't sure if this was Dr. Jekyll I was meeting and that if I went for coffee, Mr. Hyde would be joining us.

At that moment, Aunt Cathy approached me and explained that our group was getting a bit hungry and would be going to the restaurant there at the museum for a bite to eat.

"Cathy, this is Charles Blanchard. Charles, this is my Aunt Cathy. Cathy, Charles has just invited me for a cup of cafe au lait, do you mind if I join him?"

I felt more comfortable knowing my aunt and her group would be in the same room as us, so I decided to take a chance and see what this guy was like. This was a vacation of a lifetime, and so I figured I should take advantage of it. I did feel a little uncomfortable not telling my aunt about our unusual introduction, but I'd explain it later.

"Of course not, but we probably will go back to the hotel after lunch, so don't go too far," she cautioned.

"Oh, we're going to the restaurant as well, so I'll see you there," I explained hastily. I didn't want Cathy to think I'd wander off with this stranger, and I certainly didn't want my friends to leave me behind with him.

Charles ushered me out of the gallery, and I followed him to the beautiful restaurant, one entire wall of which was the inside of the face of a clock. After a brief wait, the waitress approached us and greeted Charles like a regular, even inquiring how his great-grandmere was today. That really blew me away. This must be a regular scam this guy tried on unsuspecting female tourists. I decided I was about to find out more.

Our table was wedged in the back just between the Roman Numerals four and six. Despite being a museum eatery, it had a relaxed yet at the same time intense atmosphere. French people always seem to be talking so passionately, even about something as commonplace as reminding their companion that they need to stop for a baguette on the way home. I was taking in so many experiences that for a moment or two I wasn't aware that Charles had spoken to me.

"Mademoiselle Ellen, do you wish anything with the cafe'? Perhaps a croissant? They have chocolate and raspberry filled ones. They are délicieuse! "I snapped out of it and apologetically requested a cafe au lait minus the lait and a chocolate croissant.

Embarrassed my lack of attention, I focused on my 'date' and asked "So, Charles, come here often? The waitress seemed to know you well." I gulped realizing I'd delivered yet another smart-aleck remark.

"I come here once a week to visit these paintings – they are like my children, I'm very protective of them."

I reflected on this man: he looked like he held a responsible job – perhaps as a museum guard or a businessman; handsome, I realized – now that I knew that he wasn't crazy – but apparently someone who appreciated art for more than the brushstrokes. But to be protective of the art – was this whole thing an elaborate pickup story or was I just dealing with someone with a fanciful imagination?

As I came out of my reverie, I realized that, again, Charles was speaking to me and I was embarrassed about drifting in and out of the conversation, so I resolved to enjoy the moment. Here I was in France having a croissant with a Frenchman and feeling so grown up and continental. I was hoping he didn't think I was a bad listener, but how could I politely tell him that I was taking all this in, making notes for my diary later, and then rejoining the conversation already in progress.

"So, Msr. Blanchard, are you a painter as well?"

"No, I have a much more pedestrian occupation. I am an inspector for the Sureté. However, I haven't forgotten my love of art. My main assignment is to trace and recover stolen artwork."

"My how exciting. . ." I thought to myself - 'I wonder how many he's found? It just gets better and better.'

"As a matter of fact, that is I why I come to the museum so often. I find being surrounded by all of these masterpieces helps me to mentally take on the persona of the thief and visualize how the crime happened and what kind of person did it. As you know it so rarely is the butler." - That last remark was clearly for my benefit. He wanted to know if I was still listening or if I had withdrawn into my own mental assessment of him.

"Now I understand - The protectiveness you feel for these paintings is job-related -

How interesting! How effective is your system? Do you find you're successful with that approach?"

"Well, over the years I have indeed been successful, and the job does have its rewards, free access to museums, first-rate travel to locations all over the world, but it is also very boring. You know art thieves are a very different breed. They are as a rule well educated, with good upbringings and little taste for violence. I carry a gun but rarely have had to fire it. Mostly it is like a chess game, waiting to see what move your opponent will make next."

I was finding myself drawn to this guy and I wanted to know more about him, but at that very moment, I noticed Aunt Cathy's group had stood up from the table and were preparing to leave. I didn't want the conversation to end, but I also didn't want to be left behind. While I was sure that my new Amie would be able to get me back to my hotel, I thought for practicality's sake I had better get along. So, with as much grace as I could muster, I thanked Charles for the meal and raced off to join my party. It wasn't until I was standing in the gift shop paying for a print of Whistler's Mother that I realized that I never told him that I hoped to see him again -- clear evidence of why I'm still single.

CHAPTER 5

Back at the hotel, I prepared to take another nap. We were going out for our first Parisian dinner, and I wanted to enjoy it. It had been an exhausting 24 hours, and I was pretty sure that once my head hit the pillow, I'd be out for a few hours at the least. As I lay down, I processed all that I had seen and done that day and expected at the very least I'd be having nightmares about the trip in that flying sardine can, but my last thought as I drifted off was of my new friend, Charles.

I woke up three hours later hearing my aunt tiptoeing around the room. When she saw that I too was awake, she asked me how I felt. When she told me, I'd been muttering something in my sleep about a stopping a thief who had run away with Mrs. Whistler's eggs, I felt that the time had come for me to tell her about my friend Charles.

"Well, Cathy, you know the man I met at the museum, he was telling me about these stories he makes up about the paintings there. You see," I paused here wondering how this was going to go over. How much should I tell her? Cathy was a pretty gung-ho person, but also practical and careful. She would probably worry about his stability (she didn't know him as well as I now did) and would warn me that he was just one of the characters I met on the trip and this would be a good story to tell when I got home, but I probably shouldn't spend any more time with him.

On the other hand, Cathy like the rest of my family wanted me married, and this might be the one. He was French after all, single, and he seemed respectable. She would be sure that his colorful stories were just a line he used to meet women, and that he sounded like a perfectly fine boy.

I decided to come clean and give her the chance to see it from my perspective.

"Well, anyhow, I met him in front of the painting of Whistler's Mother, and he told me that she was his Great-Grand'Mere. Oh, I know it sounds odd and don't worry – he isn't -- related but he told me about how he imagines that painting came to be painted and it was really fascinating."

"You see, he believes James made a mess of collecting the eggs one day or came home with a bad report card and his mother got mad at him; he mollified her, by painting her. Anyway, he is a police inspector, specializing in art thefts. I told him that I was staying here in Paris for a few more days, but I didn't mention what hotel I was staying at. I figured he was an interesting man, but nonetheless a stranger so I thought it would be better if I didn't tell him too much about me." My story at an end, I waited for her reaction.

"Oh! What a funny story! Why didn't you tell him where we were staying? I'd like to meet him!"

That wasn't the reaction I expected. Was I being too cautious? I certainly didn't want my Aunt to be more adventurous than I was. Now I wished I had given him a little more information.

At that very moment, there was a polite knock on the door, and Cathy who was dressed went to answer it.

"Madame," the bellman said, "we received these for your companion." In his arms was a beautiful bouquet of yellow tulips.

Cathy signed for the flowers, tipped the bellman and closed the door behind him.

I got up and reached for the flowers. "Are you sure these are for me?"

"Here is the note on the back of a business card." I flipped over the card and read the message. "May we continue to get to know each other - you've already met my great-grandmother. Charles"

I looked at the other side of the card, and there it was. Charles Blanchard... Sureté. He was a chief inspector for the famed Sureté. He hadn't been lying. I was relieved.

But wait a minute, how did he find out where I was staying? Almost immediately, I figured it out. Sure, someone who works for the Sureté probably knew what room I was in and what I had for dinner on the plane last night. The important thing was that he wanted to see me again and I would have another chance. Now I had to figure out what the next move was.

Should I call the Sureté and thank him for the flowers? It would be a good way to find out if he really worked there and didn't get a business card made up as a prop.

"There is a number here on the card for his office," Cathy interrupted, verbalizing my thoughts. "Why don't you call him to thank him for the tulips and ask him to join us for coffee at the restaurant tonight?"

"Okay, I guess that would only be polite. Where is that number?"

As I waited to connect to his extension, I seriously considered hanging up, but this little voice inside of me reminded me that he gave me his card, with his number on it. It did seem that he wanted to hear from me again-- in fact, his note confirmed it. I was just being silly.

"Allo? Charles Blanchard, how may I help you?"

"Why did you answer in English?" I asked, "How could you have known that I wasn't some French art snitch instead of me?" pausing, I realized I must've sounded like a nut. So, marshaling some dignity, I continued, "This is Ellen, I met you at the Musee D'Orsay this afternoon? You sent me flowers."

"Of course, I remember you Mademoiselle Ellen. I'm glad you received my flowers already - did you like them?" He said with a chuckle in his voice.

"Oh, I love them. Thank you very much. As a matter of fact, that's why I called, to thank you and to extend an invitation to you to join my group for coffee tonight after dinner. Would you like to come?"

"I'd love to join you. What time is convenient?" I filled him in on the particulars, gave him the name of the restaurant, apologized for not being able to provide directions, (he said he would find it) and quickly signed off.

Seconds later the phone rang. It was him. "By the way, the receptionist who connected you to me told me it was an English-speaking lady on the line--that's how I knew that it wasn't my French-speaking art snitch on the line. I expect he will call later."

"Okay, how did you get my number so fast?" was my next question. Charles' answer was prepared. "I had the number of the hotel from when I ordered the flowers. I just asked for the room of the charming, outspoken American woman who got the yellow tulips today. They immediately connected me with you."

I had to laugh, and I suppressed my next question which was to find out how he knew where I was staying. This guy was a real challenge. I could tell his wit would easily keep up with mine. I had to admire that.

"Well thank you again, I'll see you later." We disconnected, and I sat back in stunned silence. This man really seemed to like me. Cathy was standing beside me waiting to be filled in on the arrangements, so I complied.

"Mr. Blanchard will meet us at the restaurant tonight after dinner." "What do you think I should put these beautiful flowers in?" Cathy, the world traveler, spoke right up.

"I asked the bellman to bring us a vase." Cathy; ever prepared.

Now I had to figure out what to wear to dinner. I had brought dressy clothes but nothing that would do for a second cup of coffee with a French policeman. Clearly, I would have to be creative. Not having much innate style, myself, I figured that I would just match up a skirt and blouse with possibly a fashionable scarf and a conservative jacket -- the scarf would make the ensemble more Parisian.

I took a long shower and spent the time considering my options. I had brought a pair of nice, cream colored slacks, they would do, and the pale pink silk blouse with my navy jacket and a pretty floral scarf would have to suffice. Of course, I could wear a dress, but that would be trying too hard. Next time.

When I emerged from the shower, the bellman had already delivered the vase and Cathy had set the tulips in it. "Just add some water to them. I have some aspirin in my case in the bathroom. Drop one of those in, and they'll last longer. Where do you want the vase?"

Now, regardless of the fact we were staying in a nice hotel in a great location, the room was small, and despite the great view and the French windows, I was at a loss for a place for the flowers. Finally, I moved my suitcase off the coffee table and placed them there. Bon!

CHAPTER 6

A high point of every trip to France has got to be the food. Aunt Cathy and I met our group in the lobby and slowly assembled for our trip to the restaurant. The tour had included dinner at local restaurants, all within walking distance of our hotel. Becoming comfortable walking the streets of Paris doesn't take very long; the problem is just getting started. We had a map of course, and after much discussion and debate finally decided to head out of the hotel to the right and follow that to the side street where our restaurant was located. It was a pleasant walk, but I was tired and anxious for the meal to be over and coffee to be served.

Our group must have looked kind of funny -- seven older women and me. Perhaps I was taken by passersby to be the tour leader, but I was definitely a follower. I walked along next to Susan and Jessica, and they questioned me about the young Frenchman who I had coffee with at the museum that afternoon. I wasn't sure if Cathy had told them that he would be joining us later for coffee at the restaurant but figured I had better mention it.

"Well, he is a member of the Sureté, and he was in the museum this afternoon gathering information about one of his crimes. You see, he, Msr. Blanchard investigates art thefts, and he says being in the museum helps him associate with the criminal mind."

"How fascinating, tonight when I see him, I'll ask him how that works."

Ok - clearly, Jess had been clued in. When had Cathy spilled the beans? Was there some kind of network that these women were connected to and I wasn't -- kind of like an office grapevine? Jess and Susan were already looking at me with more respect. My first day in Paris and I already had a beau?

"I understand he sent you flowers." Eleanor and Laura chimed in.

Pauline and Vivian were the only ones I hadn't heard from yet, but they were lagging behind us. Vivian having lost an earring already was wringing her hands and explaining that she "had picked those out on a trip to Egypt several years ago. They were in this little market in Cairo - the vendor had tried to take advantage of me on the price, but I held out and paid a paltry sum even by Egyptian standards."

Pauline explained to her that we didn't have time right now to go back to the hotel and look for the earring since we had dinner reservations and Ellen's young man was going to meet us for coffee afterward, but we would ask the Concierge about it when we got back to the hotel.

"He isn't my young man -- as a matter of fact, he isn't even young. He's at least 37 or so!"

"But so distinguished, a police inspector!" Pauline pointed out.

Pauline was clearly taken with the whole scenario. A very well-educated woman, I could tell she had led a colorful life. But all those trips abroad hadn't conquered the romantic in her. She bought the whole enchilada.

"Perhaps the inspector could help us look for my earring," Vivian piped in. "You never know where it could be now. You know women, or tourists, really, in Paris have to be so careful. The streets are loaded with gypsies. I should have been more careful about showing off these earrings."

"I'm sure that your earring will turn up in your room, Vivian. It probably fell off when you were putting on your coat. I'm sure you would have noticed someone tugging on your ear." I pointed out politely.

"Yes, I'm sure that's what happened," Cathy added.

Finally, we arrived at the restaurant, a typical French eatery, I gathered, but it looked so much like the restaurants at home I was a bit disappointed.

We had been provided with menus as a part of our travel documents, and so we knew what our entree was to be -- in fact, we had looked up all the elements in the French dictionary and were assured that it was some form of beef.

Dinner was a garrulous affair. The women in my group were all well-educated and time was spent telling me about their various trips and anecdotes about past fellow travelers.

The next morning, we were to travel to the Normandy coast to view the site of the D-Day invasion. Much of the conversation encompassed the more practical aspects of the trip; where Serge and our bus would meet us (outside the hotel) and when (practically dawn); where we would stop (hopefully for breakfast) and when we'd return (late in the day).

Several bottles of wine were circling the table, and I'm happy to say they made their way to me on a few occasions. I was becoming increasingly nervous about the prospect of my Inspector being interrogated by my group of Miss Marples. I scanned the room, to determine what if any routes of escape were available. A couple a few tables away were gesturing wildly to a waiter who, comically, busied himself with arranging napkins on a table several feet away. The distance itself was not daunting, and it occurred to me that the waiter in question must have had a hearing deficit to have entirely missed the "allo's" and "pardonez-moi, garcons" being tossed his way.

At another table, an older man and a young boy were talking, and every once in a while, the older man would shake his index finger and utter a phrase in German. From the few words I could translate, the older man was talking about a chicken coop . . ."

The distractions served their purpose. I forgot what I was worried about until I replayed the conversation I had just heard and stopped cold at the words; 'grandmother' and 'chicken coop.' It brought me up short. We were already into the dessert portion of the meal; coffee had been served 10 minutes earlier, and still no Charles. The ladies were starting to look around in anticipation, savoring their coffee and mentally planning the insights on international crime that they would impart to him.

For myself, I was looking at being stood up on another continent, and I'll tell you I wasn't looking forward to writing that in my diary. A few minutes more and I'd just leave, and if my new crime-sniffing friend ever showed up, he could investigate my disappearance.

I passed on dessert but was willing to help finish off the bottle of wine. Eleanor and Cathy were casting worried glances between them, and Pauline and Jessica had busied themselves with figuring out the bill. Vivian kindly leaned over to me, and in a stage-whisper said, "perhaps someone turned in my earring, and he is busy trying to find out who it belongs to."

I thanked Vivian for her compassionate suggestion and took another sip of wine. When my aunt leaned over to me and said gently, "it looks like your friend is detained -

we should probably get ready to go." I decided to give up the ghost and pack it in.

I was feeling a bit sorry for myself, but not undone by this turn of events. Back at home, I would be able to brag that I had met, been wooed by and walked away from a Frenchman all within 8 hours. Surely, a record.

As we prepared to leave the restaurant, a car screeched to a halt out front and, there was a commotion at the front door. I noticed this only because the conversation around me had abruptly stopped and the ladies had turned away from their purses and wraps, to see what was happening. I had taken off my glasses earlier, and I couldn't quite make out what was happening up front, but when Jessica exclaimed, "It's a police car!" I figured, either the place was being raided, or my date had arrived.

Charles swept in and whipped off his overcoat with a flourish that only the French could pull off and made his way to our table.

"I am so sorry I am late ladies; I had a last-minute call from a colleague, and I was delayed. I see I have missed the coffee, but perhaps you would all join me in an aperitif, my treat, of course."

Charles looked my way to see if I were angry and quietly said "I am very sorry. It couldn't be helped. But I dispatched my business as quickly as I could so that I could be here. Do you forgive me? I was really looking forward to meeting your friends."

Snatching victory from the hands of defeat, *this was no longer a 'stand-up,* I graciously accepted his offer. The ladies, of course, were thrilled to meet Charles and quickly put their purses and wraps away and took their seats.

"Msr. Blanchard, I am so happy to meet you, Ellen has told us all about you," Laura gushed.

"How exciting your work must be. Was it a crime that kept you from us tonight, Msr. Blanchard? Susan queried.

"I've lost my earring, somewhere between here and the hotel," Vivian declared, "do you suppose you could help us locate it -- it's of great sentimental value. My husband Henry and I bought it on our honeymoon in Egypt 40 years ago. Henry, he's gone now, bought them for me at a darling market near Cairo, the first gift he had given me as his wife." OMG! Even Vivian was injecting romance by claiming a sentimental story for the self-described cheap earrings SHE had bought in Cairo!

Fortunately for me and I suppose for Charles as well, the waiter arrived at that moment, and the ladies became involved with ordering their nightcaps.

"I just want you to know," I murmured to Charles, who was to my right, "the only thing I told them was that you worked for the Sureté. They do not know about your familial relationships. I thought you would want to save that for the second cup of coffee. Cathy, my aunt, of course, knows, but she can be discreet," I said with a twinkle in my eyes.

Charles smiled and thanked me for my thoughtfulness and told me I looked lovely. "Ok, you win. I don't care if you're related to Empress Josephine, you're forgiven!"

Charles laughed out loud then, and I joined him. He really was a charming man and not bad looking either. I sized him up in a subtle way, and he was starting to look quite dashing to me now. Perhaps that was the wine talking. But he did have that Hollywood-European look to me.

Suddenly something occurred to me, and I glanced quickly at his left ring finger -- just to assure myself that his tardiness had nothing to do with a Madame Blanchard waiting at home. My glance reassured me that it was only a criminal that had delayed him.

The ladies had moved into the interrogation stage now and were obviously enamored. Jessica and Susan, who besides my Aunt Cathy were the most sensible in the group were peppering him with questions about past cases and not so delicately dropping hints about where we would dine the next night.

I could see that Charles was enjoying himself enormously and in no hurry to leave, so I just sat back quietly and watched the show.

Forty minutes later I could tell the ladies were tiring, and I, myself was beginning to tune out. The noise and the laughter were battling with jet lag, and I needed some air. Charles, as if sensing my change in demeanor, announced to the ladies that he was sure that they were weary from the trip and he had a busy day ahead of him and needed to take his leave of us. He gestured in a very continental way for the waiter, who zipped to his side and produced the bill with a flourish.

I think the ladies were glad of the interruption in the festivities and thanked Charles (they were all calling him Charles now - "Inspector Blanchard" had departed with the first round) profusely for the drinks and said they hoped we would see him again -- soon!

I hoped so too. I had to admire the man for being able to keep up the pace of conversation he had, after spending the day keeping the world safe from art thieves.

Charles helped me with my coat and asked if he could escort us back to the hotel. The ladies, now anxious to be in their beds (we had an early call in the morning, I remembered) had sprinted ahead, which was nice since I really had had no time to talk with him alone since earlier in the day at the museum. As I shrugged into my blazer (unaccustomed to masculine assistance), a grey-haired gentleman bumped into me, and I dropped my purse, the contents spilling out over the floor. Charles, ever the gentleman, settled the coat on me and bent down to pick up my possessions.

"Oh, please let me get those – I know where everything goes." My protestations were quietly ignored, and Charles finished gathering all my items and stood up. The grey-haired man who had collided with us was gone without offering an apology. "Mademoiselle, I apologize for that gentleman – the French are nothing if not polite. Obviously, he is not one of us." With that, Charles escorted me from the restaurant and toward my hotel.

It was a nice night for the states, but in Paris, it was divine. The moon was visible over the Tuileries Gardens, and as we walked along, I reflected over the events of the day.

It was enough to be in Paris, but having Charles along as my police escort, put this in my diary as tops. We talked quietly, and he asked me about myself but, I don't really like to talk about myself, which is definitely a drawback to making new friends.

"Well, not really much to tell, I come from a fairly large family, I live with my parents and work every day." As I mentally recited this boring biography, I was tempted to embellish but decided that one of us with a fictional past was definitely enough.

"My family lives in a small town outside of Boston, and I have a busy job. I work for an accountant, as his assistant. I don't prepare taxes, but I do all of his computer work and prepare presentations for large prospective accounts. It's a paycheck. I have several nieces and nephews and keep busy on the weekends seeing my friends and doing the things I don't do during the week. Pretty boring stuff, huh?"

"Not so boring. It sounds like a nice normal life. Did you always want to travel?"

"I never really thought about it very much. I have made the usual trips with my friends to Florida, and Washington, DC, but beyond all that, except for some business travel, I really haven't been anywhere. So, when this trip to Paris came up, I really thought about it -- for about 30 seconds and agreed to go. Boy, was I lucky that I had that severance pay or I would never have gotten here!"

"Severance pay, I'm not familiar with that term, what is it - you lost a limb - got a divorce? What do you mean?"

"Severance pay," I explained with a chuckle, is what they call it when the company you work for is taken over, and they want to replace you with someone of their own or reduce staff. They pay you to go! So, I guess, in my case they did me a favor - they paid for my trip to France, after a fashion."

"So, this accountant, he replaced you and paid you to go?" Charles was getting confused, and I can't say I blame him. His biggest problem was one or two or perhaps as many as three well-educated criminals trying to do him in. I had had a Fortune 500 company nipping at my heels.

Chuckling, I went about explaining that the job I had now was a new job and that the severance payment was compensation from being laid off from my previous one.

"Do you like your new job?" Charles inquired.

"Well, it's stable, keeps me busy, and it pays me -- not well, but enough to keep me comfortable. I like my new boss, and I think the new company is small enough to rule out any hostile takeover bid."

I didn't want to talk about things as ordinary as work. The mood was romantic and the thought of slogging to work on another rainy New England day was a downer. I also couldn't help but feel that the comparison between Charles's career and my daily grind was at best like comparing an apple to a pomegranate. One was sensible and homey, the other exotic and juicy. This evening clearly called for something less mundane. I didn't want to be predictable and ask about his cases, but on the other hand, I was dying to know. By the time I had made up my mind to be nosy and ask, we were standing at the entrance of my hotel.

"Well, mademoiselle, I have really enjoyed this evening. Your companions are delightful, and I think they are rather fond of you. They will take good care of you when I cannot. I must say good night now. You have an early call in the morning.

Charles reached out and took my hand, and for a moment I almost threw the arm and the rest of the body with it. I didn't want to say good night or Bon Nuit or Bon Chance or anything else but "When will I see you again?" but I refrained.

"I enjoyed myself as well, and I apologize for being so sarcastic at your expense and for boring you with my work talk. I also want to apologize for the ladies. They were just getting into the spirit of the evening, and I hope they didn't bother you too much. You see, I'm sure they see this as just a great adventure. I'll hear all about it tomorrow and the next day. You've certainly made their trip!"

I didn't want to add, *and mine as well*, but I was thinking it. As we were standing there, nothing more passing our lips, the silence was deafening until a strange beeping started. I was momentarily confused until I realized that it was Charles' cell phone ringing. He reached into his jacket and withdrew the offending object; the item that had put off an awkward moment - the goodbye, for at least the moment.

"I must take this call. Let's go inside off the street, and I'll take it there."

I followed him intrigued and a bit annoyed. I had high hopes for that moment of silence, but this was interesting. *What crime was occurring? Was this his snitch, was he going to have to jump into a taxi and ride out of my life before I gave him my home number?*

Charles had by this time pulled me into the hotel, still holding onto my right hand.

He softly unclasped our hands. *Was mine holding that tightly?* and drew me beside him while he returned the call. We were touching but only hip to hip. It was enough. He spoke a few words in French to the person on the other end and quickly bid his party adieu. I was dying to know what had transpired and asked as soon as he had hung up the phone.

"Was that your commander? Has something happened?"

"Yes, it was my boss, and I fear I must leave you. I've had some information I have been waiting for, and I really must see to it immediately."

He drew me to the elevator, his hand gently beneath my arm.

"I will see you to your room and then I must go."

The elevator was a tiny thing, really only suitable for just two and it fit us close enough so that when I turned to wish him well, we were only inches apart.

"I'm sorry I have to leave so abruptly, but I will see you again, I hope?" he inquired.

"Of course, we'll meet again. I can't wait to hear about your adventure tonight."

Charles nodded, and of course, I knew that he wouldn't be able to tell me the good stuff, but he didn't say so. Instead, he just tipped my chin up and leaned down and dropped a very soft, sweet kiss on my lips. It was enough for the moment.

"Will you be safe?" I asked a bit plaintively.

"Yes, I told you, Ellen, my line of work is very safe, very pedestrian. Nothing to worry about."

The elevator doors opened and, I stepped out.

"My room is just across the hall. No need for you to leave the elevator. Bon Nuit," I said quietly.

I let go of his hand and stepped out of the elevator. I watched as the elevator door closed and stood there in a daze for a moment. I slowly walked across to my room *really only just a few steps* and paused for a moment before I opened the door. I wasn't ready for the moment to end. I knew that by opening the door and crossing the threshold the evening was over and so was my brief romantic flirtation.

CHAPTER 7

Charles hastened back to the restaurant a block away, where he'd left his police car. The information he had received he'd been waiting for. Charles had been investigating the threat to steal a Renoir painting from the D'Orsay Museum. His source had told him that he was approached to propose a switch. In exchange for a valuable work of art that had been stolen 10 years before, Charles would make it possible to allow him access to the D'Orsay, where the Renoir hung. If Charles did as he was instructed, and the thief was able to gain entry to the museum without alarms, the missing

Childe Hassam painting would be left for him in a safe place, and he would be notified of its' location.

As unusual as the request was, Charles was contemplating allowing the swap. Of course, he would never let the thief leave the D'Orsay with the Renoir, without a tail, but he must take a chance. The Hassam was Charles' only failure during his tenure at the Sureté. Taken 10 years ago – the Hassam was stolen from the Louvre and was Charles' second case on the job. Despite exhaustive investigations – even as recently as this year, Charles was never able to solve the crime. The trail remained cold until two weeks ago. That was when his informant had brought him this proposition.

Initially, Charles had vehemently turned down the proposal. He sent the informant away with the French equivalent of "Hell no!" ringing in his ears. But he couldn't put the thought out of his mind. The Hassam was a precious and valuable painting and one that the French Government wanted back.

And, Charles wanted a chance to solve the one case that had eluded him. He had proposed to his superiors that they make a copy of the Renoir and hang that in place of the original at the d'Orsay. His superiors and the director of the museum were more afraid of hanging a fake Renoir for the public to adore than they were that the original would be stolen. Charles was told to arrange the swap and see to it that he got both paintings back.

Charles had tried to contact his informant but had waited more than a week and, until tonight, had not a single lead. The information he'd received in the call from his commander was welcome. His informant had been spotted in a town on the northern coast of France. Charles would make his way there and try to make contact.

His only regret was that he had to leave Ellen abruptly. He was immediately attracted to her wit and openness. She was lovely – curvy, unlike his countrywomen. Her chestnut hair framed a pale, lively, Irish face and her enthusiasm for all things seemed like a breath of fresh air to him. Frenchwomen were elegant and controlled, as was his life.

The moment he saw her gazing with amazement at the Whistler, he knew he had to meet her. So, he used the story about his great grand-mere to tweak her interest. Finding out where her hotel was, was easy. Her companion, Vivian, as he now knew her, had a brochure in her hand from the Hotel St. Jeanne when they left the Musee D'Orsay. So, as soon as he returned to the office, he'd arranged the flower delivery. He had hoped she would ask him to join them that evening, and she did. *I wish it were this simple to track down Marco,* he mused as he got into his police car.

CHAPTER 8

The streets of Paris were wet the next morning, when I boarded the bus for Arromanches. The night before was still a soft memory to me, and I thought I'd doze a little and replay it a bit during the ride to the Normandy Coast. But the ladies were wide awake and curious about my walk home with the enigmatic inspector and were anxious for details.

I briefly described the short walk home and avoided any embellishments, as much as I knew the girls would enjoy it. Instead, I turned the conversation back to the reason for our early rise, deftly avoiding describing the moments in the elevator.

We, as I mentioned earlier, were heading for the coast of France, where decades earlier the famous D-Day invasion took place. I had never followed the history and stories of WWII very closely but being here in France had piqued my interest in it. Having put the subject on the table, I withdrew to my thoughts and let the ladies hash it out. The French countryside was beautiful, and I settled back to watch it pass me. After 45 minutes or so, we pulled off the highway to refuel, and the ladies mentioned walking over to the restaurant for a cup of coffee and a croissant.

The restaurant (it would have been a Roy Rodgers or a Burger King in the U.S.) was on the other side of the divided highway, approached by a covered walkway that traversed the road. Inside, we inquired about the facilities and, in turn, each made a visit. I was last out, having spent a precious few minutes trying to figure out how the unfamiliar toilet facilities worked. There seemed to be electronics involved and, wary of electrocution, I finally used the handicapped restroom, which fortunately was low-tech.

When I returned to the dining room, the ladies were seated around the counter ordering croissant and coffee. I had not eaten the breakfast provided by the hotel that morning, preferring hunger to the dry toast-like crackers or the French version of Twinkies. As a result, I was quite hungry and happy to settle down with a cup of joe and a buttery croissant. The croissant was fresh from the oven and dripping with butter, and the coffee was plenty hot and plenty black. I had declined milk, I felt it watered down the caffeine and today I needed it.

Vivian, uncharacteristically, I thought, had ordered a Chocolate Croissant, and a cup of Hot Chocolate. Later on, I thought, she would be racing from one beach to another and driving us all crazy with the folklore. For now, I was content to watch her licking her fingers and exclaiming in delight about how delicious and fresh they were and to wonder what my friend the cop was up to.

Aunt Cathy, who had been asleep when I got in last night and wasn't able to question me in our rush to get ready this morning, sat down beside me and asked how my evening had ended. I mentioned the call that Charles had received and that he said he hoped I would see him again soon. *Me, too.* I realized that I had used up one of my four days in Paris and the clock was ticking.

Serge came in at that moment and announced that we needed to get going. I reluctantly set down my still-hot cup of coffee and joined the others in the cold gray French morning.

I settled myself back on the bus and prepared to doze for the next hour. As I listened to the ladies talk, I realized something Charles said the night before was nagging at the back of my mind -- something about the ladies taking care of me when he could not. *What, I wonder, did he mean by that?*

We reached our first destination at about 10:30 am, the D-Day Museum, a striking building on the edge of a hillside. As I waited for the others to join me outside the bus, I was moved by the beauty and significance of the many flags flying against the cloudy gray cold, sky. How magnificent and how perfect! I could almost hear the drone of the airplanes and the thunder of thousands of feet hitting the beach.

There were photographs of fresh-faced young men -- most of whom, I mourned, hadn't returned. Especially fascinating was the interactive exhibit that told the story of what happened that day from both the Allied and German perspectives.

After an emotional morning at the museum, we re-boarded the bus for the short drive to Bayeux, where the famous tapestry was housed in an ancient cathedral.

Lunch was at our own discretion and Cathy, and I chose a quaint little tea shop where, besides another man, we were the only patrons. Cathy enjoyed an omelet and tea, and I tried my first Croque Monsieur and tea. We talked a while about what we saw. Cathy reminded me that my Uncle William had flown a general during the invasion, making it so much more real to me.

After lunch, we boarded the bus for a trip to the beaches. It was a frigid April day, and the cold sea air seeped into my bones. The vista from the small seaside museum we stopped at was breathtaking. Later we went to Omaha Beach, which still resonated the moments and hours of bloodshed that had taken place decades before.

As I predicted after watching Vivian fuel up at breakfast, she was running from battlement to battlement, pointing out to Laura the "Mulberries" – artificial harbors installed by the allies during the invasion. At one point she wandered a tad too close to the edge of the cliff, choosing an area not enclosed by fencing. Pauline and Jessica along with Susan were shouting to her to be careful. I assessed what was happening and quickly sidled up beside her and grabbed her arm.

"Vivian, perhaps you should step back – I don't think you realize how close you've come to the edge," I pointed out, and she quietly complied.

"You know, my brother was here that day," she said. "I'm sorry, I guess I got a little carried away. I've always wanted to come here. He's still here. He never came home. His name was Victor."

I looked up at her, and her face was very drawn, and her eyes closed. Her mouth moved a bit like she was praying or saying hello. I gave her a minute, even though I was freezing from the wind and rain, and then suggested it was time to go. I gave her a little hug around the shoulders and guided her back to the bus.

A visit afterward to the American Cemetery reinforced in me the reality of what had happened on those long-off days. I felt tears well up and run un-interrupted down my face when I read one gravestone declaring that the site marked the grave of one 'known but to God', and I was humbled and grateful. And I thought of how lucky we were that Uncle William had lived to fight another day and how sad it was that Victor and thousands of others like him, hadn't.

After the cemetery, the ladies and I, much quieter now, took the bus to the nearby city of Arromanches to do a little souvenir shopping.

As we waited at the curb for our group to reassemble (a few had crossed to the stores to purchase postcards) I noticed a small silver car pass by, going rather fast for such a small street, so crowded with tourists, followed closely by a black Audi, traveling at a similar speed. The second car slowed to allow Laura to cross the street and I couldn't help but be struck by the driver's resemblance to Charles. Laura darted quickly to the side of the road, and the black car was gone, but not before I spied the distinctive antennae on the back of the vehicle. It was a police car, and I wondered what my dashing inspector was doing in a town like Arromanches, so far from Paris.

The ride back to Paris was quiet. Just about all of us were occupied with our own thoughts. Myself, I was wondering if it would be too forward to invite Charles for coffee again if he were back in town, or if I should just let it go. Chalk it up to a lovely evening that I would tell my grandchildren (or more likely my grand-nieces and nephews) about, many years down the road.

CHAPTER 9

The doldrums of the afternoon immediately dissipated after spending some quality time under a hot shower. I was feeling a bit more like myself, again mentally scanning my wardrobe, keeping in mind that tonight didn't have the importance of the night before; no Frenchman was going to buy me a cup of Java, but I was in France, and it wouldn't do to underdress.

I stepped out of the shower and toweled dry. Cathy was already napping, and I didn't have the heart to wake her, so I quickly dressed and exited the room as quietly as I could. I had chosen a pair of wide-legged navy pants with a tiny polka dot pattern, a white ruffled blouse and a canary blazer. Not haute couture, but it would do.

I boarded the tiny elevator and pressed the button for the 1st floor. I thought I'd walk along the street and window shop for 15 or 20 minutes. Late afternoon was quiet along the Rue de Rivoli, and I had the sidewalk pretty much to myself. I peered at the wares in the shop windows and found a perfume store that seemed intriguing, so I went in. Minutes later I emerged, smelling I'm sure, like (you should pardon the expression), a French whore, with a new bottle of Joy and a lighter purse.

I had paused a moment to make sure that I had placed my wallet back in my bag when I was struck from behind and knocked to the ground. My attacker grabbed my bag and in the resulting confusion, managed to trip and fall, landing his heavy body on my left arm and sending pain up through my elbow to my neck it seemed. I screamed or continued to scream *actually, I'm not sure if that screaming, I'd been hearing since the onset of the attack was my attacker or me*. Fortunately, I had carried an umbrella with me, and it found its' way to his gut during the tumble to the street.

Seconds later, a weight was lifted from me, and I found myself alone, my upper torso on the sidewalk and my legs and lower half lying in the gutter. Two shopkeepers ran from their stores and with a passerby, tended to me. The purse snatcher was long gone, and so was my purse, identification and my new bottle of Joy. Well, most of the Joy was gone anyway. There was a puddle beside my right breast, and the aroma wafted up to me along with the smell of the street. The combination of scents finally overcame me, and at that moment I passed out.

I awoke in a hospital room, surrounded by my ladies. Cathy was sitting beside me holding my right hand. I felt an unfamiliar stiffness on my left and realized that my left shoulder was immobilized.

Vivian, Laura, Eleanor, and Jessica were standing nervously at the foot of the bed and Susan was desperately trying to question the nurse about whether the police had been by.

Cathy, noticing I was now awake, patted my good arm and asked me if I was in a lot of pain. I nodded and tried to keep the tears that were welling in my eyes, from dripping down my cheeks and onto my neck. I was in a great deal of pain, but I was also very groggy. I guessed that they had doped me up and I decided not to complain about it.

"Honey, your shoulder was dislocated, but they managed to reset it. Thankfully, you don't have a concussion, but the doctors want to keep you overnight for observation."

"No. I won't stay overnight. I want to go back to the hotel. I'll be fine. Just have the doctor prescribe some kind of painkiller, and get me out of here, I won't spend one of my four nights in Paris in a hospital bed!"

"Ellen, dear, I don't think that's a good idea," Jessica warned. "The doctor said you may have a delayed reaction and experience some confusion."

"I'll be fine. Please just ask the doctor to discharge me. I will feel much better just getting back to the hotel and getting in my own pajamas and lying in my own bed. Really, this is not where I need to be. I promise, if I start humming La Marseillaise and speaking Russian, you can call the doctors to come and get me. But, in the meantime, all that's wrong with me is a sore shoulder and wounded pride. Let's get out of here!"

Cathy looked at me maternally, and I guess reluctantly decided to trust my judgment. "Ok, we'll get you discharged, but any funny stuff and I'm calling 9-1-1 or whatever the French version of that is."

The doctors clucked and scolded, but in the end, my ladies stuck up for me and pressed my case. They would keep a 24-hour watch if they had to and would call an ambulance at the first sign of erratic behavior.

My canary blazer was a mess, and my blouse as well. I finally left the hospital in a blue-gray johnny tucked into my slacks. A bra wasn't possible with my new accoutrements, so I went without.

The wheelchair took me to the sidewalk, and an orderly helped me into a waiting Mercedes taxi. *What style!* And I learned to appreciate the smooth ride only a Mercedes could deliver on the trip back to the hotel. The driver cautioned at two-minute intervals that I had just been mugged and seriously injured, managed to treat the accelerator with a bit more respect, and presently we arrived back at the hotel.

Since it was still early, Cathy and I encouraged the ladies to keep our reservation at the restaurant, since dinner had already been paid for. I was in no shape for dinner out. Cathy and I would order room service and get to bed early.

After a lengthy, painful, (for me) debate, Vivian, Laura, Eleanor, Jessica, Pauline, and Susan agreed to go to dinner but would be back early to relieve Cathy and keep watch over me. (I mentally planned to be out cold by then.)

We saw the ladies off; me from a perch on a chair in the lobby and heard them cautioning each other to be careful; they didn't want to be the next victims on the trip.

Cathy helped me to our room, and we settled in. My pretty jewel purple silk nightshirt wouldn't fit over the sling, and I didn't want to butcher it, so I just slipped off my ruined slacks and settled back on my pillows.

"Do you feel at all like eating?" Cathy inquired gently.

As a matter of fact, I was hungry, and I said so. Cathy ordered what she knew to be my favorite meal, Filet Mignon, mashed potatoes and a vegetable. A salad would have been a bit too difficult to manage, and so she decided against that. For dessert, a simple chocolate cake (if the French ever made anything simple) and a glass of iced tea. I had suggested wine for dinner, but Cathy pointed out that I was taking some high-octane painkillers and probably shouldn't. She ordered a scotch and water for herself.

"I'm sorry Cathy, I guess I've really ruined your trip. All I was doing was window -shopping. I didn't think that was dangerous. Did the police have anything to say about who may have mugged me? He got my purse, you know, my passport, fortunately, was here in my suitcase, but he got all my money and my credit cards and my bottle of Joy."

"Honey, you haven't ruined my trip, don't be silly. The police are investigating but held out little hope your bag would be found. I wonder if I should have mentioned that we are acquainted with Inspector Blanchard. Perhaps that would have helped put a little emphasis on the investigation. Thank God that you left your passport here, that would really have been messy."

"Tomorrow, I'll call home and see if they can wire me a few hundred dollars. That should be enough."

I tried to settle myself a bit more comfortably against my pillows and grimaced a little. Cathy offered to get me some more of the painkiller the doctors sent me home with, and I allowed her to. I was beginning to ache again and fortunately at that moment, dinner arrived.

Dinner was delicious but a challenge for me to eat. I was exhausted at the end of the meal but determined that I wasn't going to go to sleep at 9 pm in Paris.

Cathy pulled chairs over to the window for us and opened it up, and we propped our feet on the windowsill and watched the moon over the Paris skyline. It was a perfect evening, except for the throbbing on my left side and the smell of Joy invading my nostrils.

"Aunt Cathy? What do you think of Charles? ...er I mean Inspector Blanchard?" I was shy talking about him, but I really liked him, and I wanted to know if I was being blind to some character flaw.

"Oh, I think he's lovely -- quite a gentleman, and totally hot! Isn't that what you'd say? He reminds me of Richard. Lovely."

A moment went by while I processed this before I said "Richard?"

Aunt Cathy's voice got softer, and I could tell she was wrapped up in memories that she wasn't sure she wanted to share.

"Richard Long was my fiancée back in 1945. He died on VE Day." Cathy's voice trailed off.

"I've never heard you mention him before. Why now?" I tried to keep the surprise out of my voice.

"Well, I suppose that being here in Paris has something to do with it... And Charles looks very much like him, so that's part of it, but mostly I think it was the trip to Normandy that had me thinking about him." We met here in the summer of 1937 on my first trip abroad. And we spent a great deal of time together here and at home. He sent me a letter proposing to me on D-Day. I've never forgotten what he said.

"I've seen many lives ended here today, Cat, and I'll never forgive myself if I don't tell you how much I love you and how much I want to marry you. I beg you, marry me! Give me something to look forward to... Something to think about while I lie in ditches."

"I said yes, and we planned our wedding for the first summer after the war. We sent plans back and forth by airmail and military post. Richard was an architect, and each letter was full of sketches of the home he'd build for us in New York. "It was exhilarating and emotional for me. I loved him very much, and I've never found anyone better." Her voice full of emotion, Cathy continued.

"Richard died on the way to Paris. His transport truck crashed en-route to the celebration marking the end of the war. I received a letter from his commanding officer explaining what had happened."

"So, that was my true romance - he was the love of my life, and he gave me the time, of mine. I can only hope Charles is yours. I like him very much."

Momentarily speechless, I swallowed two or three times and wiped the tears from my eyes with the cardinal red napkin that came with our dinner trays. I measured my words.

"You know, I've known you all of my life, but I just realized that I haven't known you for all of yours. I wish I'd met Richard, but I'm glad you did. And I'm very sorry he died. Thank you for telling me about him."

"Ellen, let me say one more thing...you are a kind, lovely person yourself, but you have an acerbic wit and a tendency to pre-judge a situation. This time, knowing how nice Charles is and knowing what happened to me, loosen up a little. Let Charles romance you. This next couple of days could be making an extraordinary memory for you."

I could see that Aunt Cathy wanted to move off the topic, so I changed the subject.

We talked quietly about the attack and moved onto the trip to Normandy we had taken earlier in the day when our reminiscences were interrupted by a knock on the door.

Cathy got up and answered the door. It was Charles, and he and Cathy spoke quietly for a moment.

"Ellen, I heard about your accident. Are you okay?" I could tell that he couldn't see me from his vantage point behind me, but as he came around, light dawned, and his face became ashen.

"I'm fine, just a sore shoulder. It won't keep me from enjoying the rest of my trip. But how did you know? Did your police colleagues tell you?"

"No, as a matter of fact, I went to the restaurant where you were dining, and the ladies told me. I'm sorry something like this happened to you in my city. Normally the streets of Paris are very safe. Sadly, though it only takes one person to ruin that image for tourists like you."

"I really am fine. Strangely, I wasn't scared. I always thought that if something bad happened to me, I would be too frightened to react, but I wasn't. Actually, I had the presence of mind to jab my attacker in the stomach with my umbrella. I bet he'll be eating only soft food for the next few days!"

Charles had taken Cathy's seat next to me and was leaning forward with his hands clasped in front of him. He looked urgent and concerned, I suppose because he isn't used to the violence in crime. His cases as he has said a few times are usually more challenging to the mind than to the body.

"Tomorrow I shall see what they have found out, and I will take you to the store to pick out some clothing you can wear with that new accessory of yours. The Galleries Lafayette, are close by and will have plenty of things to choose from."

"That's very kind of you, "I said groggily. My head was beginning to droop, and I was starting to see two Charles', and no Aunt Cathy. "Where is my Aunt?" I asked faintly.

"She went to the lobby to see her friends. They're gathered down there trying to figure out the next couple of days. You won't have too much energy for sightseeing so they are trying to figure out what you can do as a group." I was overwhelmed by the generosity of everyone.

These women, most of whom I barely knew, were tailoring their holiday around my limitations. Charles was going to take me to get new clothes and help on my 'case'. It was too much for me, and as I sat there in my hospital johnny, with filthy matted hair and reeking of Joy, the tears started to slide down my cheeks. It was bad enough having Charles see me this way, but the tears wouldn't do.

"I'm sorry, Charles, I'm all of a sudden very tired. I think I will go to bed now. Please excuse me." I got up somewhat shakily and started to sway and almost knocked him over, but he caught me in the nick of time and helped me to my bed. The room was so small he didn't have to drag me very far. I lay down as gingerly as possible on the small twin size bed, and then he gently covered me with a blanket and shut out the lights. The last thing I remember was him looking down at me and murmuring something about Paris not being the city of tears.

CHAPTER 10

When Charles left Ellen he was angry. He knew that she was going to be alright, but seeing her bruised and battered, and tinier than he could imagine, made him wish that he was the kind of cop who could track down purse-snatchers and dole out a little justice. He knew that he was overreacting but the thought that someone walking down the Rue de Rivoli in broad daylight could be so injured woke something in him that demanded to be made right.

He left the hotel and returned to the police station where he inquired about the attack. Det. Lt. Boutin, an old friend, and former partner told him that it was just a random attack and the only funny thing was that they had found her stolen possessions behind the hotel – intact!

"How odd – there was money in the wallet – her credit cards were there?" Charles asked.

"Well, of course, she'll have to identify everything, but it doesn't seem to be disturbed," Boutin answered.

Charles thanked Boutin and left the station with more questions than answers.

The next morning, he determined to himself that he would make this up to Ellen and called his friend Francoise who operated a boutique. She was willing to open early for him, and he went on a bit of a spending spree.

CHAPTER 11

I tossed and turned all night reliving my moments on the Rue de Rivoli, and screaming for the thief to stop.

When I awoke, the room was awash in sunshine, and I could hear the shower running. Cathy was obviously up early. I took a moment to ascertain how I felt and realized that with the minor exception of a dull throb, I was ok. My head felt a bit thick, but otherwise, I seemed to be in pretty good shape.

What an entry for the diary this would be. I wondered briefly, egocentrically, if the papers back home would have any news coverage about the brutal attack of the beautiful young American tourist outside her Paris hotel. The article would mention of course that she bravely fought off her attacker and that an inspector of the Sureté was involved in the ongoing investigation.

That reminded me that I really should call my folks and let them know I was all right, before the State Department notified them out of the blue.

I smiled to myself at this fantastical daydream and shook off the remnants of my drug-induced stupor. I got up gingerly and sat for a moment at the edge of my bed trying to accustom myself to a sling on the left side of my body. I remembered that Charles was taking me shopping today and that's when I also realized that I had nothing to wear and didn't know how I was going to wash my hair or the rest of my bruised and filthy body.

Cathy emerged from the bathroom at that moment and greeted me.

"Good morning honey, how are you feeling? Are you in much pain? I probably should get you one of your pain-killers before you get moving about too much."

"I feel ok. Perhaps a bit stiff, but otherwise fine. My biggest challenge right now is trying to figure out how I'm going to get cleaned up and what I'm going to wear today."

"Well, if you're concerned about your appearance, I guess you're on the mend. The doctors said you shouldn't move your arm too much, but I suppose you can take a bath and I'll try to wash your hair over the sink. Shall we give it a try?"

"Yes, sure, but what am I going to wear? Would you mind opening my suitcase for me?"

I used my left hand to dig around in my bag and came up with a sundress that wouldn't require too much movement of my left arm. The problem was that it was only April and I was pretty sure that I wasn't going to be very warm wandering around in nothing but a sleeveless cotton dress. Luckily, I had thought to pack a light cotton cardigan which I figured I could throw over my shoulders. Having pulled together today's wardrobe, I got up to make my way to the bathroom when there was a knock on the door.

Really, we had a lot of company for a couple of American tourists so far from home. I thought to myself.

I declined to answer the door but instead sent Cathy for it. I really was going to have to get her a nice gift for waiting on me and putting up with me on this trip.

It was Charles, and he greeted us warmly. Cathy got the two-cheek kiss, and I suppose because I smelled a bit greasy, I got an air kiss, which I managed to catch with my good hand and plant on my lips *not my cheeks as I was sure was intended.*

"Charles has come bearing gifts, Ellen. He has been shopping already and has solved your wardrobe problem." It was clear, that Cathy was impressed with this generous gesture, as was I.

"How nice! I assure you that as soon as I receive my wire transfer from home - *I needed to call about that, soon,* I'll reimburse you."

"No need Ellen, it was my pleasure. This is the least I can do to make up for the barbaric treatment you were subjected to yesterday. Let's see, I asked the woman at the store to recommend some things for someone who is unable to dress her left arm, and this is what she suggested."

Charles withdrew from the bag, an adorable sleeveless tee, with thin white stripes on navy. A cotton cardigan in white piped with navy and a pair of navy slacks.

"I figured that since it's chilly, at the least, you could put this sweater on over your top, and it would keep most of you warm. I also took the liberty of picking up this dress for you to wear tonight. You will look tres' chic."

I was astounded. Charles had picked out a lovely strapless linen dress in the softest shade of pink, with a small rosebud in the center where my cleavage would be. Very strategically placed. He'd paired it with a hot pink cashmere pashmina.

"Oh, this is far too generous of you. I couldn't possibly accept." I was astounded at the kindness of this man, who only 2 days earlier I had mentally thought could be psycho.

"I know that you want to clean up, so why don't I meet you downstairs in a half hour and we will decide what you will do today." Charles was taking this role of protector, a bit far, but I suppose there are worse things than getting travel tips from a native, so I meekly complied.

"Yes, and I must make a call home and arrange for that transfer also, so it will probably be more like 45 minutes. I hope you don't mind the wait. Of course, if you have to be somewhere, we will understand completely. You have been more than kind."

"That reminds me, I checked with the department, and your purse has been recovered. As a matter of fact, it was found in the alley behind this building shortly after the attack. Later on, I will take you down there to collect it."

"Oh, how wonderful! I'm sure there won't be anything left in it, but it will be good to have it back all the same."

"Happily, the purse appears to be undisturbed. There is money in the wallet, and I saw some of the things I remember picking up from the restaurant floor the other night."

Charles took his leave of us then, and Cath and I set about making me presentable. It wasn't easy, but I managed to get all but my injured arm clean with the minimum of mess, wash my hair and dry it. It was when I looked in the mirror, that I really saw the damage my attacker had done. I had a bruise under my right eye, and my nose was scuffed. There was also an abrasion on my forehead, and I realized that in the last twelve hours, Charles had really seen me at my worst. *He must really feel bad for me,* I thought.

I set about making a silk purse out of a sow's ear. Makeup would hide most of the damage, and I decided to wear my hair down rather than back in my usual headband, to hide the mark on my forehead. The bandage would be somewhat visible, but that couldn't be helped.

After I spoke with my parents and reassured them that I would live, Cathy and I collected our things and made our way down to the restaurant where the rest of our group was undoubtedly grilling Charles.

The ladies all cooed and clucked over me when we got to their table and insisted on going up to the buffet and getting me some food. Apparently, they thought I needed my strength because they came back with plates laden with fruit, the ever-present croissant, coffee, eggs, and juice. It was much more than I ever would or could eat at breakfast, but I didn't say a word, so touched was I by their caring. Charles sat beside me and offered to help organize my food but having him scoop fruit into my mouth was not something I was willing to do.

"No, really, I can manage. Please just relax. You've done enough."

"Ellen, we thought if you were up to it, we'd take a bus tour of the city this morning, then you could come back for a nap, and this afternoon, we'll take a leisurely stroll around the Louvre. How does that sound to you?"

Jessica was thoughtfully mapping out the most comfortable route for me to see Paris and the wonders of the art world and I was very grateful.

"It sounds wonderful -- I'm dying to see the Louvre! First, however, I must visit the Sureté and collect my purse. Is that convenient?"   I looked at Charles for his agreement.

Charles nodded his approval and reached to pass me the coffee he had refilled.

Since he was on my left it was awkward for me to grasp the coffee and I jerked my right hand over to grab it, and in the transfer, managed to send my fruit salad skimming across the plate and onto Charles's lap.

I was mortified. "I'm so sorry. Here, let me help clean up." Charles just laughed and grabbed the nearest napkin and daubed the offending mess away. Most of the strawberries and cantaloupe had slid right off his dark pants and landed on the floor.

"My pants are fine. It could have been much worse. I could have had hot coffee spilled instead. Don't worry about it. Now, finish your coffee, and I will take you downtown."

Cathy was coming with us, and the rest of the group was going to walk around the area -- together they assured me, and perhaps wander through the Tuileries Gardens, for the hour or so that it would take us to complete our errand.

I wanted the ladies to resume their own interests, but they insisted on waiting. Jessica had obtained a schedule for the tour buses and assured us that they were adequately timed so that we could get one when we returned. It occurred to me that I never found out from Cathy how she knew about my attack the night before and I asked her about it now.

"When I woke you weren't in the room, and so I dressed and came downstairs and met up with Vivian and Laura. We were in the lobby when the Concierge was notified that someone had been knocked down on the street and so we went out to see what had happened. My heart was in my throat when I recognized your jacket and slacks on the body on the stretcher. Thank goodness I had Laura and Vivian with me to rally the troops. I rode in the ambulance with you and prayed that you were all right. The rest of the group joined me to wait with you at the hospital. What a terrifying experience! I'm so glad you're okay. Do you really feel all right, because we could put this trip off until later?"

"Yes, I'm fine, and I'll be much better when I reclaim my bag. Let's find Charles. I really don't know what we would have done if it weren't for him smoothing the way. And all of you have been wonderful, I'm very grateful to have such friends."

Charles had gone to arrange the car, and he met us in the lobby. Soon we were on our way to the police station.

At the police station, we were directed to a department on the second floor, and Charles introduced us the Detective Lieutenant Boutin, who had custody, I assumed of my belongings.

He produced my purse from his desk drawer and politely asked me to identify it and check for missing belongings. I looked through the interior and confirmed that it contained my wallet and the money that I had been sure was long gone. Everything else seemed to be there, my license, pictures and all of my credit cards, which lead me to wonder -- out loud, why it had been taken in the first place.

"We wondered the same thing mademoiselle when we looked inside. It seemed that nothing had been stolen. Do you confirm that?"

I spilled the contents out onto the desk and peered through them. "Yes, everything seems to be here - isn't that funny, a matchbook -- I don't remember having any matches with me. I'm not a regular smoker, so why would I have had them?"

I picked them up, and the detective took them from me and commented on the car rental agency advertised on them. It was a French firm, and I confirmed for him that we were traveling by bus on our trips out of the city and didn't rent a car at any time. Charles took the matches from the detective and examined them. On the inside of the lid were three words '2am - Mardi - D'O.'.

"That isn't mine, how odd. Do you suppose it's a clue to my attacker?"

"Most probably, Mademoiselle or I suppose there is an off chance that these matches were dropped on the Rue de Rivoli by a passerby. The most likely explanation, however, is that your attacker in his fall dropped the matches and when he grabbed everything to get away, he also grabbed the matches. We shall give it to our squad to investigate. What do you suppose is meant by D'O?"

I looked at Charles and could almost see the wheels turning in his head. D'O to me in my limited experience of Paris meant only one thing - the Musee' d'Orsay. I knew that Charles was thinking the same thing - what was happening tomorrow night at the museum at 2am?

I suppose that there were many other sites in Paris whose name began with D'O or perhaps many people. But when talking of crime in Paris, the first thing that came to mind was art.

I wondered if Charles would share his suspicions with his colleague. But as the minutes wore on and I answered questions regarding the attack, Charles was very quiet. I figured he was worried about the family masterpiece and thought I would mention it to him later.

After another 10 or 15 minutes, the detective finished his questions, and then he and Charles spoke in French for another minute or so. Even though Charles had assured me, and I had confirmed, that my possessions were intact, I was still mystified by the attack.

We were dismissed after Charles, and his police associate finished their exchange. As we walked out of the station, I could tell Charles was deep in thought.

He saw us to a taxi and apologized for not being able to accompany us back to the hotel. I told him I understood completely and that we had taken too much of his time already. I thanked him for everything he had done and wished him well in his investigation. As Cathy was getting into the taxi, I took a moment to ask him about the significance of the matchbook found with my belongings.

Charles brushed it aside as a nothing piece of evidence and assured us that his evidence team at the department would leave no clue un-investigated. He added that since matches were such a commonplace item in any city, let alone in Paris where everyone smokes, that it wasn't unusual to find some with appointments written in them.

"But an appointment at 2 am? Don't you think that's kind of an odd time for an assignation? Who besides cops, thieves, and bakers are awake at such an hour?"

"Ellen, please let me handle my business, and you worry about enjoying your trip and healing quickly. I appreciate your interest and will let you know if anything turns up, as unlikely as that is."

It seems I was just given the brush off, and masterfully. I nodded coolly and told Charles I was sure the evidence was in good hands and said goodbye.

As I settled somewhat awkwardly into the taxi, I noticed that Charles had already disappeared into the building. I hoped he would forgive my cool goodbye. It also occurred to me that he had said nothing further about seeing me again and we were leaving in two days.

CHAPTER 12

Our tour of Paris was thrilling, but for me, exhausting. I had taken another painkiller when we returned from the Sureté, and it kicked in as our bus rounded the Place De La Concorde. I'm sure that Marie Antoinette and her Louis would have been glad to have what I had as they were facing the guillotine on that very plaza. That said, Paris was the most beautiful city I'd ever seen – despite seeing it dulled by painkillers.

When we passed the Arc de Triomphe, it occurred to me that I probably should have asked Charles to take the dress he had bought for me, back. It was too dressy for any of the tourist-level restaurants we'd be visiting, and I didn't want to be beholden to him. The dress and wrap certainly must have cost a good deal, and if I didn't wear them, it would be a waste. But I wasn't going to wear the dress tonight and look so out of place among my group and fellow tourists. I would call him when we got back and suggest I return it for him.

I was happy when the bus returned to the drop-off spot, not because it was an arduous trip but because I was eager to make my phone calls and take a nap.

The walk back to the hotel was very brief, and I felt much safer in the group. Eleanor and Laura had been trading anecdotes about their first visits to Paris and how awestruck they had been by her beauty. Vivian was complaining that she never seemed to get a window seat on the bus and had missed almost everything.

Cathy was walking slightly ahead with Jessica and Susan and sharing a laugh over some incident on the way. Cathy had taken my bag, and it swung from her shoulder as she walked along. I rushed to catch up with her to let her know I wouldn't be going to lunch when I heard a squeal of tires and saw a small red Renault approach the same crossing Cathy was. Cathy was about to step into the path of this speeding car. I yelled at her to stop and elbowed aside the couple who were walking along just to the front of me. Fortunately, Jessica and Susan saw the car just in time and managed to pull Cathy out of its way just before it would have struck her.

When I reached them, Cathy was laughing nervously and thanking her two friends for acting so quickly.

"Cathy, are you all right? That car almost hit you! These crazy French drivers aren't careful at all. He came out of nowhere."

I thought it was a bit odd considering that the traffic was relatively light and saw no reason for the driver to be going so fast. He couldn't have been impatient with the other drivers since there were so few and the chilling thought I had was that he must have seen Cathy stepping into the street and deliberately didn't stop. I shook off my worry and took Cathy's left arm in my right, and we set off on our trip back to the hotel.

Once we returned, we went directly to our room, stopping briefly in the lobby shop for a newspaper. When I pushed open the door, I felt a slight vacuum, as if the door had air pushing against it and it was tricky to open. Once inside the room, I figured out the problem quickly. The two French windows were open, and the room was turned upside down.

Cathy and I were too stunned to speak. Both of our suitcases were open, and the contents were spilling out; many were on the floor. The beds were rifled, one of the mattresses was even partway off of the frame. The bathroom was in a similar condition. Our makeup bags were dumped on the sink, and my mascara had fallen into the open commode. Even my loose powder was spilled out, and the empty box was on the floor.

I finished my inspection, expecting that Cathy was right behind me, but as I turned towards the bedroom, I saw her quickly rummaging through the chaos of our belongings.

"Cathy, what are you doing? I don't think we should touch anything until the police get here. You may be damaging fingerprints."

"I'm looking for our passports," she commented in a tight voice. "They are not here!"

"I'll call the front desk. Don't worry we can get new passports quickly. Thank God we weren't here! You don't suppose this was the work of a clumsy maid?" I joked awkwardly.

"No, this was most definitely not the work of a maid. I just can't understand what they were looking for. Can you?"

"I don't know Cathy, but it just seems that since I met up with Charles, I have had more encounters with the police than I have in all of my thirty-something years. Do you suppose it has something to do with Charles?" My question was meant to be funny, but I couldn't help the feeling of unease I had.

After calling the hotel desk to report the ransacking and now with the specter of our missing passports -- the robbery, I sat down weakly in the only chair free of debris. The hotel detective was on his way to the room, and he would notify the police should it be necessary. I wasn't sure that I should put the responsibility for my ability to return to the states in the hands of the hotel, but I would wait and see what he said. I was reluctant to call Charles again, for fear of further involving him in our unlucky lives.

Minutes later the Hotel Manager and the Hotel Detective arrived and pronounced the room a mess! I, of course, could have told them that, but courtesy held my tongue. The detective felt that we should report the robbery immediately and offered to do so. I complied, reluctant to call the station myself. I had just been there a few hours ago retrieving one of my stolen belongings, I really didn't want another consultation with Detective Lt. Boutin today. In the meantime, we would be given another room.

The manager was most apologetic and couldn't understand how something like this could happen. I could, however. We were on the second floor, not really that far from the ground, so if the perp didn't enter via the door, he probably could have gotten in the window. At least it looks like he got out that way. And Cathy and I hadn't seen another soul on our floor since we checked in several days before. The other ladies were together on the third floor, and we had been separated because there were no further vacancies on that floor. Chances are that the thief had chosen our floor because there was so little foot traffic on it.

I needed to use the facilities and was reluctant to use the toilet with the evidence of our heist still in place. I asked the manager to show us to our new room, and he went for the key.

Fortunately, he was quick about it, and he told us in the elevator on the way to the fifth floor that he had a beautiful room for us. And he did.

The room was actually a suite, and it was very Parisian.

There was a sitting room with a wall of windows and a balcony with chairs and a table. The two bedrooms and bathroom that would make Martha Stewart green with envy. The sitting room was beautiful. Painted a pale butter yellow, with white trim and lovely floral furniture, a wet bar (which we were urged to take advantage of -- "it's on the house, we are so sorry.") I only hoped the suite was as well. I asked, and the hotel manager nodded his assent, eager for us to forget the sight of our room downstairs.

I remembered that I had to use the bathroom and shyly asked Cathy to give me a hand getting organized. The hotel manager left us, and we completed our business and went back down to our old room to see if we could collect any of our belongings.

The hotel detective answered the door and let us in. The tables, windows, suitcases and bathroom fixtures were covered with a fine white powder. I wondered if they would be dusting our clothes for fingerprints as well.

I poked my head into the closet and noticed for the first time that my new dress was still there. *Well at least the perp didn't have a flair for fashion,* I mumbled to myself. I debated on how I would go about returning it without contacting Charles, but I didn't have to ponder for long. As I pulled my head out of the closet, someone knocked on the door, and one of the army of rookies powdering my room went to answer it.

Naturally, the first person to walk through the door was my personal crime fighter, Charles Blanchard, followed closely by Detective Lt. Boutin.

"Mademoiselle, you must be the unluckiest tourist, I have ever met!" The lieutenant exclaimed.

"Ellen, Cathy, are you both all right? That's becoming a common greeting between us," Charles chuckled.

"I know. My arrival in Paris seems to have spurred a crime spree. Our luck has even spilled onto the streets. First my accident the other day, and today Cathy was almost run down by a car!" I love Paris, but I'm beginning to think we should get out of town before we get killed."

"I'm beginning to think all of these incidents are related," commented Charles. I was beginning to think so too, my only disappointment being the eerie connection to my meeting with Charles.

Something flashed in my mind at that moment -- the speeding car in Arromanches and the car following, whose driver bore a stunning resemblance to my new protector.

"Were you in Normandy on Sunday? "I asked without pause. Charles tried to avoid the question with a remark about seeing to the investigation.

"Please wait a moment. Were you in Normandy on Sunday? I demanded. "I saw you in a car, and it looked like you were chasing another car that almost ran Laura down. I'm sure it was you. Was it?"

"Yes, as a matter of fact, it was. I was in Arromanches on a tip, and the man I was looking for got away in that pursuit you saw. I stopped to let Laura cross, and he was gone, how do you say, in the blinking of an eye?"

"Why didn't you mention it to me? I've seen you since, yet you didn't even mention the coincidence."

Charles drew me out of the room at that moment and closed the door. "I don't want to worry you, but I don't think that or the attack on you or the near-miss with the car or, this latest incident are coincidences at all. And, that is why I am here. To protect you and to get to the bottom of this.

"What could I possibly have to do with this crime wave? I've only been in Paris three days and the only person besides shopkeepers, hotel and restaurant personnel and most recently, medical people and policemen, I have had any contact with is you!"

"I am not sure, but something tells me this must have something to do with my investigation."

"But you told me yourself that art thieves have very little penchant for violence, and I think it's getting violent."

There was an inner excitement in me that may have had something to do with the proximity of Msr. Blanchard, but it also had a lot to do with the raw thrill of being involved in an investigation of a crime.

Nothing this interesting had ever happened to me before. The adrenaline was pumping through my veins, and I felt as energized as you can be when you're recovering from a mugging and sporting a sling.

"What do you think we should do?" I questioned Charles.

"I don't think we should do anything," he explained. "I will continue with the investigation, and you will see France, with a bodyguard of course."

"How can I possibly sightsee, with a bodyguard shadowing my every step?"

"What if it were me?" Charles asked quietly. I'll be very well behaved and will only act if I have to push Vivian out of the way of a bullet or protect you from another marauding purse-snatcher. I promise, and I am an excellent guide. In any case, you really don't have any choice."

I was beginning to see that, and actually didn't mind the possibility of spending the next few days with Charles, but I felt I should make some kind of token protest.

"I am a grown woman. I can take care of myself, and I don't know if the rest of my friends will be willing to have you along."

"I know that they will love my company. The ladies, as you call them, are thirsty for adventure and this will give them something to brag about for the next year. Not to mention the fact that they are already planning our wedding. Why just last night they told me how perfect I was for you and that they were pretty sure you didn't have any other romantic entanglements. Oh yes, I'm sure they won't mind my being along."

This conceited diatribe was succeeding in reddening my face. I could barely speak; I was so mortified. I couldn't believe the ladies would betray me this way. But part of me was flattered and not a little pleased that Charles had taken up the gauntlet that they had dropped.

"Well as long as you behave yourself and don't mind carrying all the bags. That reminds me. We're scheduled to visit the Louvre this afternoon. I hope you don't see that as a busman's holiday", I commented with a touch of sarcasm.

"Oh no, not at all! I know it well, and I will make sure you see everything you need to. Now, let's see if they are done, we'll collect your things, settle you in your new room and get you a brief nap before our trip to the Louvre."

I almost asked if this new role of his as a bodyguard involved joining me in my nap.

CHAPTER 13

After my brief (solo) nap, I tidied up. Cathy was in the sitting room, talking on the phone with the American Consulate about our passports.

I stumbled out with my shirt out of my pants, no shoes and a severe case of bed head. It was at that moment that I noticed Charles standing at the window. But, before I could gracefully withdraw to the bathroom to clean up, he turned from the window and said, dryly, I thought, "Good afternoon, sleepy head." An apparent reference to the state of my hair.

"I'm sorry, I didn't realize we were entertaining," I fired back. "I was on my way to the restroom. I'm not familiar with the layout of this place. Pardon me, I'll be right back."

I made the most of the time in the bathroom and almost didn't want to leave. I was embarrassed at being caught, again, looking like a drowned rat and not the sophisticated Americaine I was sure that Charles expected.

When I left the bathroom, I was feeling much more presentable and had resolved to make the most of having a bodyguard.

Cathy was off the phone by then, and I asked her about the results of her call.

"It will take at least three more days to get new passports, but in the meantime, we will be issued temporary ones. The only problem is that we can't leave the country without our new ones, so I guess we're stuck here in Paris for the rest of the week!"

Stuck in Paris, what a mixed message that was! Despite all that had occurred here, I loved every bit of Paris and wasn't a bit sorry to have to spend more time here. Not to mention the fact that I would have more time to spend with Charles and could perhaps see this investigation through to its conclusion.

"Well, I don't mind that, but what about the ladies? Will they go on without us? What about our arrangements?"

"I have already spoken to Jessica, and they are all thrilled to be staying. Although they are disappointed to miss most of the London part of the trip, they are looking forward to the adventure of seeing France through Charles's eyes. As for our accommodations, Jessica has contacted the hotel in London and arranged for our arrival on Friday. The hotel here had given us this room free for the next few days and arranged for a discount for the ladies. The travel company is taking care of their bill out of the savings on the London bill. So, we're all set."

"Well then, perhaps we should be getting on to the Louvre," I said, ready to go and test out this bodyguard thing.

"Don't you want some lunch? You hardly had any breakfast, and with the pills, you're taking I really think you should eat something." Charles was wasting no time in exerting his newfound influence over me.

"No, I'm not a bit hungry, and it's almost 3pm. We won't have time to see much before we have to come back and get ready for dinner. Aren't our reservations for 7 o'clock?"

"We have changed the reservations. Charles is taking us to an elegant restaurant, he says, for dinner and our sitting isn't until 8:30. Rather late, but for such a special treat, I don't think anyone will mind waiting." I could tell that Cathy was intrigued and excited and I couldn't help but be excited as well.

"What restaurant is this? Is it famous? What will I wear?"

"The restaurant is well known, but a surprise. I won't divulge the name of the restaurant. We'll just arrive there. And, you have the new dress I brought back for you today, so your wardrobe is not a problem. That reminds me. We haven't done anything further about getting you more clothes which will be more in fitting with your injured arm. If we have time after the tour, we'll run over to the Galeries Lafayette and see what we can come up with for the rest of your trip. Now, if you are sure you don't want lunch, perhaps we should be going. I believe the rest of our group was to meet us in the lobby at 3:15, so we better get organized."

As guaranteed by Charles, the ladies were indeed waiting and all atwitter with the prospect of a tour of the world-famous Louvre, by this man whose job, among other things, was to protect the treasures between its walls from modern-day pirates.

"Oh, Charles, we are just so excited about this trip. Most of us are familiar with the Louvre, but to see it from your perspective will truly be memorable." Vivian was, I could tell caught up in the suspense and adventure. I am sure that she, like the others had this vision of us being followed around the Louvre with Charles, by wanna-be art thieves and foiling a heist of some famous masterpiece. I didn't want to disillusion her, but I was sure that Charles's job did not follow him on routine trips to the museum. I mean, bakers, bake, even in their off hours. But an art cop didn't bring his work home with him, hopefully.

The Louvre, even with the gigantic glass pyramid designed by I.M. Pei, was an impressive structure. I preferred the older classic buildings, felt that the new entrance was a bit out of keeping with the ages-old artifacts that it enclosed, but it was, nevertheless striking.

I was awestruck when we traveled the halls of this monument to the arts and caught my breath when I looked up and saw the pure beauty of the Winged Victory of Samothrace standing alone, on the landing of a stairwell at the end of a long corridor.

This ancient statue had such beauty and grace, and I knew I would remember this vision forever.

The ladies had gathered behind me and were equally open-mouthed. After a few moments of silence and reflection, we stirred quietly and proceeded to climb the stairs guarded by this extraordinary gatekeeper.

The museum was thrilling and just about everything I saw more than met my expectations. My only disappointment was in the Mona Lisa. The painting was much smaller than I'd expected and was partially obscured by a vast crowd. The crowd here was much larger than any other I had seen to date, all of them peering at this small painting of enormous value.

We spent another hour wandering happily around the museum, but at 4:30 Charles declared that we had shopping to do and that Cathy and I would have to meet the ladies later at the hotel. The ladies were disappointed that their personal tour was ending so soon, but I wasn't. I was a bit overwhelmed with all the sights I had taken in and wanted time to process it all. We arranged to meet later and made our way back through the pyramid.

Charles hailed a cab, and as we were getting into it, I heard an alarm sounding in the general direction of the museum we had just exited.

Charles's ears perked up, and his demeanor became quite tense.

"What is that noise?" I asked. "It sounds like a fire alarm. You don't suppose the Louvre is on fire do you, how terrible!" Cathy was quite worried; her friends were still there, and she feared for their safety.

"I'm sure it's nothing. The Louvre has a very sophisticated system of security and most likely what happened is that someone tried to open one of the alarmed doors and it set off the system." Charles had regained most of his composure, but I could see a lingering tenseness in his bearing.

"Listen, I want you and Cathy to come back to the pyramid with me, and I will find you someplace to sit while I find out what has happened."

Charles dismissed the cab, and we retraced our steps to the museum entrance, where he put us in the care of a uniformed officer while, after showing his credentials, he was taken to the interior of the pyramid by another cop.

Cathy and I sat on the bench we had been directed to, and the officer stood beside us silently. After 10 or so minutes, we noticed people starting to trail out of the museum quietly at first, but as they reached the fresh air, beginning to talk excitedly as if they knew the gravity of their momentary captivity and relished their freedom.

We watched the exiting crowds and finally saw our small group. Jessica and Susan were ushering Laura and Eleanor and Pauline along, and every once in a while, would stop the group to wait for Vivian to catch up. Vivian seemed to be unaffected by the recent event and was peacefully walking along and reading a brochure she had picked up on her way out of the building.

"I was so frightened! The alarm sealed the doors, and these security people came along and ushered us all down this back hallway. We weren't searched, but we were looked over up and down as we came out, " blurted Susan, clearly affected by this turn of events; announcing that she was going back to the hotel to have a drink then take a nap.

The rest of the group were chattering excitedly and offering suggestions about what had taken place to put the museum in a lock-down.

"Do you suppose someone tried to steal something?" Laura offered.

"No, I think it was a smoke detector. Someone probably tried to light up in there" Pauline commented.

"Does anyone have a Kleenex? My glasses are so dirty, I can hardly read this brochure" declared Vivian. She was evidently undisturbed by the abrupt end of her tour.

"Where is Charles?" Jessica was the first to notice his absence.

"He's gone inside to find out what happened. He's been gone a good twenty minutes or so. Do you suppose we should ask about where he is?" I was becoming a bit concerned and was also intrigued by the incident and wondered if it had anything to do with our 'case'.

"Don't you think that someone should go find out what Charles is doing?" I asked our silent sentinel. "Perhaps he is looking for the ladies and doesn't realize we've connected with them. Why don't you go in, I'm sure they won't let me? Tell him we've found them." The guard only nodded and continued to stare fixedly ahead, apparently only willing to take orders from the man who had assigned him to us.

The ladies made noises about heading back to the hotel, and that pronouncement prodded our protector into the only words he had spoken in the time he had been with us.

"Non, Mesdames, the inspector would like you to stay together, and here we will stay. Please be patient."

That was it. No one was going anywhere until Inspector Blanchard returned.

The ladies made little noise about the denial of their return to the hotel. Instead, like the well-bred and polite women they were, they settled themselves on various benches nearby and in eyesight of the pyramid and the guard. They talked quietly among themselves, and I sensed an undercurrent of excitement in them. Obviously, this was the most exciting thing ever to happen to them, and they didn't want to break the spell.

After another ten or fifteen minutes, Charles emerged from the museum and hurried over to us. He spoke quickly in French to the guard and then to us.

"Ladies, I am sorry to hold you up like this, but now we may go. Shall we return to the hotel and relax a bit until dinner? I will take Ellen to the Galeries LaFayette for a bit of shopping and we will be back by 7 pm. That should give us enough time to get ready.

I wanted to ask about the incident in the museum, but Charles's demeanor didn't invite any interrogation. I would wait until later when we were alone or perhaps after dinner when he had had a few drinks. By then he should have relaxed and would be ready for a few confessions.

The guard escorted us to the hotel and Charles, and I bid adieus to the ladies and hopped into a cab for our shopping trip.

The Galeries were a girl's dream. I was watching my money but managed to find a few items that would suffice for the balance of the trip. Buying clothes in France is a daunting experience. You kind of have to suppress your sense of practicality and go for style -- their style. I felt like a mannequin. Trying on clothes much different than I would ever wear and with an attitude I never possessed. It was almost like remaking yourself. The French women wore clothes with such, well really attitude, and I was a bit worried that this fill-in wardrobe would look out of place and foolish on me.

But as I tried on garment after garment, I saw a different Ellen in the mirror. One more confident and stylish, than the everyday Ellen. It was very exciting -- and very expensive.

After purchasing a few pairs of linen pants, a few short-sleeved blouses roomy enough to go over my sling, and two dresses, I was exhausted and exhilarated. Charles left me in the care of two very involved saleswomen for a few minutes while I paid for my purchases and when he returned, he handed me a small gaily decorated bag and said,

"Mademoiselle, for your courage and as a reward for your lack of whining, I hope you will accept this small gift."

It was a bottle of Joy. I almost cried.

CHAPTER 14

Charles was concerned. The number of incidents involving this group of women was becoming alarming. He realized that his failure to communicate his desire to allow the art swap to his informant had forced Marco to make a new plan. That plan clearly involved Ellen and her friends.

His frustration in Arromanches on Sunday, when he stumbled on his dying informant had eased when he heard someone exiting the back of the house. He had pursued the man but had lost him when he stopped to allow Laura to cross the street.

Now Marco was using Ellen to get to him. Charles had no doubt that the attack on Ellen on the street was intended to get his attention. He remembered the first night at the restaurant when someone bumped into Ellen while he was helping her with her coat. Were the matches from him? Was that an older, grayer Marco? Then, to have Ellen attacked on the street. Clearly, he had been sending a warning to Charles. A point which he'd proven by breaking into and ransacking Cathy and Ellen's hotel room. The racing car that almost ran down Cathy and the false alarm while they were all in the Louvre were warnings. 'Be careful – I can get to her when I want!'

Yes, Charles had gotten the message loud and clear and now he worried that he could not adequately protect them.

Beyond that concern was the feelings he was developing for Ellen. He had never met anyone like her. She was shy but outspoken; courageous, yet unsure of herself. He also worried that time was running out for her in France, (and perhaps that was a good thing – by leaving France she should be out of danger). Her group was scheduled to go to England on Friday; he may never see her again.

He made a few calls on the way back to his apartment to change for dinner. Boutin had been checking on the matchbook found in Ellen's purse, but naturally, it divulged no new information. His second call was to his superior. Arrangements had been made to allow for the D'Orsay Museum door to be unlocked on Tuesday at 2am – as the matchbook had instructed. The painting had been flagged with a tracking device so that Charles could follow Marco, and a team would be in place in the D'Orsay to ensure that was all that was taken. The problem was – he had no way to let Marco know the swap was on. Unless Marco forced the issue!

CHAPTER 15

The ladies were assembling down in the lobby, and I was still trying to get over how good I looked in the dress Charles had purchased for me. I looked like a new person, even considering the sling and my assorted bumps and bruises. Cathy was patiently waiting for me as I twirled around; looked at the back and then at the front; stepped back from the mirror and got up really close. It was by far the most stunning dress I had ever worn.

I was kind of intimidated by myself. I wasn't sure I could pull off this glamour thing, and at first, I wasn't even going to wear the dress, but Cathy convinced me that Charles expected me to, and I would be insulting him by refusing to do so. Not that I minded being so glamorous, but it did take a little getting used to.

"Okay Ellen, I think you look marvelous, but we better get going. We'll miss our reservations." Cathy said with a bit more gusto in her voice.

I knew that she and the other ladies were excited about our dinner plans. Charles had been very secretive about where he was taking us. We had been scheduled to dine at another fine restaurant chosen by the tour company, but the concierge efficiently took care of changing those arrangements to the next night for us.

We arrived in the lobby just as Charles was entering. He hadn't left us unescorted all day except for the hour or so in our rooms. It was just enough time for him to go home and change as well. I suppose I should have been worried or at the least, concerned about his feeling that we needed to be guarded, but I had other things on my mind.

My arm had been okay all day, but after trying on clothes and generally moving about as we had, I realized that by late afternoon the dull throb I had become accustomed to was more like a constant knife-like ache. I didn't want to spoil the evening for anyone, so I didn't tell Cathy and quietly doubled up on my painkiller when we returned to the hotel. By the time my limited toilette was complete, the painkillers had kicked in, and I wasn't feeling even a twinge. No wonder I had seen a whole new me in the mirror.

"Ok ladies, I have arranged for two cabs. They are waiting at the curb and have been instructed where to go. So, shall we get started?"

Vivian, never happy with where she was seated or otherwise situated, was the first in the front cab and I was glad to see it. Charles guided Cathy, Eleanor and me into the second cab and got into the front seat next to the driver.

That was just as well. Here I had gone to all the pains of getting dressed to the nines, in the dress he gave me, wearing the perfume he gave me, and he hadn't said even a word to me. I was becoming a bit miffed and was trying to think of an offhand way to say that he shouldn't flatter me so when he leaned over the back seat of the car and complimented Eleanor and Cathy on how nice they looked. Then he turned to me and said "I imagined you would look just as you do in that dress. I chose well." I was stunned.

He said nothing further, and I squirmed a bit in my dress and bit my tongue to keep from condemning him for his blatant arrogance. The dress does not make the woman, the woman makes the dress, and he knew how angry it made me too. It was almost as if he were trying to pick a fight with me.

Cathy and Eleanor were gazing out the windows of the cab taking in Paris at night, which is a sight that normally would fascinate me as well, but I was so angry that I didn't even notice.

Great! This was one of the few nights I would have left in Paris, I was more glamorous than I had been in my life and he chose this moment to show the side of him I had convinced myself did not exist. Well, I was going to do something about that.

"Charles, would you mind terribly taking me back to the hotel. My arm is throbbing, and I really just want to get out of these uncomfortable clothes and lie down."

"You're not feeling well? Why didn't say anything earlier?" he questioned.

"Ellen, dear, if you don't feel well, I'll go back to the hotel with you and we can order dinner in the room." Cathy offered.

"No, I really just want to be by myself. I'm tired, and I want to stretch out and nap. I'm not a bit hungry, and I do not intend to ruin your meal by keeping you in. I'll be fine. Please turn the car around, driver and take me back to the hotel."

I kept my gaze directed out the window beside me as we rounded the Place de la Concorde and, in the distance, I could see the Champs Elysées and the glittering trees along the avenue. The Eiffel Tower winked at me as we turned to head back away from it along the Seine.

The driver, as commanded, returned us to the entrance of the hotel where Charles got out as well and asked the driver to take Cathy and Eleanor to meet the others.

"Aren't you going too?" I asked. "I'll be just fine. I just want to be left alone."

"As you know, I am not only your escort for the evening, I am also guarding you. I will see you to your room and will wait with you until Cathy returns and that is it."

"Look, I'm releasing you from your responsibility to me. I am a grown woman, and I certainly can get myself to my room and put to bed without assistance from you. The bad guys are at home having their own dinner and won't be bothering me for hours. Please go."

"As I just said, I am not going anywhere." Charles was determined, and so I relented for the moment but knew that as soon as I could, I would get rid of him.

The taxi driver was waiting to be paid, and while Charles was distracted, I slipped away. I knew he would go looking for me in my room, so instead, I went back out onto the street.

I didn't want to face him now. I was so disappointed in how the evening was turning out that I just needed to be alone. In front of me, across the street were the Tuileries Gardens and I headed for them. Just inside the gardens, I found a fountain, which faced the Seine and a five-star view of the Institut de France and the d'Orsay Museum, beautifully alight.

I sat on the edge of a fountain and remembered a few days ago, meeting the quirky policeman, and I began to cry. Not big sobs, just sad tears that wound their way down my face onto my neck. I didn't bother to brush them away. I felt like a good cry. I was owed one. It was apparent to me that the man who I momentarily considered a likely contender for the role of my husband had turned out to be nothing but an arrogant Frenchman, more impressed with the good selection of a dress, than how I looked in it. Not only had he let me down, but I had also been attacked in broad daylight, in the most romantic city in the world.

"Well, here you are. What are you doing in the park at night? It's dangerous here. Don't you know that? Are you crying? What could be so terrible?" Charles drew alongside me and crouched down so he could see my face.

"How can you ask that? I got myself all dolled up in the dress you gave me, wearing the perfume you bought for me -- I'll never look this good again, and you have the gall to congratulate yourself on the choice you made. You never once told me how nice I looked, and I did it all for you!"

"Oh, Ellen! I'm so sorry. I reacted that way because you took my breath away, but I never meant to hurt you. When I saw that dress in the shop window, I imagined how glorious it would look on you, so I had to buy it. And when I saw you come into the lobby looking like my daydream come to life, I couldn't express myself. Please forgive me."

I just sat there with my mouth hanging open. I never expected this reaction from the sedate man beside me.

"I know, the French are known for their arrogance. I would hope that on this one occasion I could be forgiven for being momentarily so tongue-tied that I chose the wrong way to express myself. And furthermore, you have done more crying than smiling in the last few days, and that simply is not allowed in Paris."

Charles was crouched down in front of me, clearly at a loss with my reaction to his apology, but for myself, after the toxic level of painkillers I had taken, and the fact that I hadn't eaten since breakfast, all I could do was laugh and cry.

I laughed with tears running down my face, and the more perplexed Charles looked the harder I laughed. Finally, as I caught my breath for a moment, Charles grabbed my good shoulder and silenced my laughter with his mouth. The kiss was unlike the light sweet kiss of our first night together in every way. There was a definition to it like the kiss was fulfilling a destiny. Not only to quiet my laughter but to silence a desire that had been building in both of us for two days. My laughter subsided, and I contributed to prolonging the kiss, as did Charles until my tears had dried.

"Charles, I apologize. I'm afraid I am guilty of many things this evening; accusing you of being ungallant; complete vanity; not to mention self-pity. So please forgive me and take me home!" I stood up quickly, too quickly and regrettably, came crashing down on Paris' answer to Hercule Poirot. As he grabbed onto me for protection, we toppled over and landed smack dab in the middle the fountain.

So there I was entangled with a man -- not just any man but a detective in charge of investigating art theft -- who, by the way, has just kissed me to a fare-thee-well -- in the middle of a fountain, in the Tuileries Gardens, in Paris, in the middle of the night and I thought to myself - sore arm and all, I am having the time of my life!

CHAPTER 16

The glamour of it all started to pall, when I realized that it is not at all romantic to be soaking wet in the middle of an algae-encrusted fountain on a chilly April evening -- be it Boston or Paris. After disentangling ourselves and a silent debate on my part about whether I should just continue apologizing for myself, we stepped out of the fountain and shook off.

"Ellen, as a man who has lived in Paris all his life, may I just tell you that I have never, ever, found myself in a fountain with a young lady. I can thank you for that new experience. Now, I suggest that we get you changed and then I will run home and change as well. I will have to ask you to accompany me, however, since I cannot let you out of my sight," he said and then quietly, "I can't imagine it."

I meekly followed Charles across the street to our hotel, ignoring the looks from the doorman, and inside to the elevator. I kept my eyes downcast, remembering our moment two nights before and the changes since then.

At the door to my free suite, Charles held out his hand for my keycard, and I took it out of my pocketbook, tried to dry it off on the front of my dress, and stepped aside for him to open the door.

I stepped self-consciously around Charles to enter the suite, where the lamp beside the big chaise cast a romantic tone over the room. The light drapes at the French windows drifted on the breeze coming in from the street. Charles followed me in, in silence, both of us too nervous to speak, or too anxious that the spell of this starry night may be broken by any utterance.

As I stood there, in this heated silence, I became aware of a steady drip. I moved further into the room, Charles just behind me, and the drip was joined by a splosh, squish, splosh. Only then did I realize that those noises were coming from Charles and me, and as I turned around and really looked at Charles for the first time since we left the gardens, I became aware of his disheveled appearance. His shoes were oozing water with every step he had taken, his typically, beautifully combed hair dripping down his face and then I noticed something glistening at his cuff. I bent down to get a closer look and realized he had a euro caught in his trouser cuff, apparently acquired during our misadventure in the fountain. Laughter started to bubble up silently from my toes it seemed until I was rocking with mirth. I just imagined what our family portrait would look like with the indomitable inspector, my husband, standing beside me, his wife, both of us dripping wet, hair matted to our skulls, in all our finery and I couldn't control it anymore.

"Oh, we're so pretty" I chuckled. My hysteria got deeper as I noticed I was kneeling in a puddle on the floor and I lost my balance, toppling over onto the floor. Charles, apparently realizing that he had a situation on his hands but not missing any of the mirth himself, reached over to grab me, spilling water out of his jacket pocket, hitting me in the eye. In an instant he was on the floor as well, laughing as hard as I, obviously overcome.

After a few moments, our giggles subsided, and I found myself staring into eyes staring into mine. I leaned forward to meet him in a kiss, knowing he was thinking the same thing when Charles' cellphone started to shrill or perhaps gurgle was a more appropriate term. The spell broken, I managed to get myself up off the floor, while he answered his very wet phone.

"Blanchard here, who is this? Can you say again? I can't hear you... Yes . . . Yes, now I understand. I will meet you there. No, of course, I will come alone. Please. . . Be gentle with them. Yes, 2 AM, I understand. Adieu." Charles, who, only moments before had been laughing with me had gone white. Once he hung up the phone, he ran his free hand through his wet and matted hair and started pacing and muttering to himself in broken English, interspersed with a smattering of what I could only assume were French four-letter words.

"What is it, Charles? Can you tell me what's happened?"

"Non. Go change into something else. You 'll catch pneumonia. I must make a call." Charles dismissed me as if he were removed entirely from me.

I quietly slipped out of the room and into my bedroom. As I awkwardly changed into my new black linen pants and a black silk shell. I ruminated over Charles's odd behavior, and I wondered what was going on. I turned to the task of making some sense out of my hair -- fortunately, curls, curl, when wet, so I didn't look too bad.   After straightening out my makeup and spritzing a bit of Joy to mask the scent of the fountain, I slipped into some flats and exited the bedroom. Charles was nowhere in sight, but I saw the drapes by the French doors blowing and realized that he had gone out onto the balcony. I got a bottle of red out of the honor bar and grabbed a couple of glasses. With the wine bottle in my sling and the wine glasses in my free hand, I slipped out through the French doors to join Charles.   He was smoking, leaning over the rail.

"I brought some wine. I can't open it, but if you will, I will hold the glasses while you pour. Charles? Is everything alright? You haven't been the same since the phone rang."

"Here, Ellen, let me pour that wine. I am afraid you will want it once I tell you what I have to tell you." Charles's face was drawn, and as he took the bottle out of my sling, a sad smile crossed his face. He poured the wine and handed me a glass. Then he directed me to a chair. I sat down apprehensively, and he knelt in front of me.

"Charles, you look so serious. What is it?" My throat was suddenly dry, and I took a sip of my wine preparing myself to be told something awful. Like he was going to have to leave me because his wife had just been released from the institution and he was needed. Or that he had contracted some terrible hard-to-pronounce disease and that he needed to go to Geneva for treatment. But when he finally told me, I was the one who needed to run.

"I am so sorry. That phone call was from a man I know as Marco. He has apparently been following me and therefore, you, and has obviously been the cause of all of your trouble since arriving here."

"Tonight," he paused, "Tonight the driver of the taxi that you, and I and Cathy and Eleanor got into was a man who works for Marco. They never arrived at the restaurant. He is holding them hostage because he wants me to let him steal something. In exchange, he will return a piece of art which was stolen 10 years ago. He wants me to meet him somewhere tomorrow night at 2 AM. If I allow the exchange then, he will release your Aunt and her friend. If not . . ." his voice trailed off. He spoke again, slowly, dispiritedly, "I am so, so sorry. I did not foresee this. I never expected that that . . . bastard would use you and your friends to get to me. But I promise you I will get them back!"

I had no words. My hand holding the glass began to shake. Wine sloshed over my hand and onto the patio.

"What do you mean, he has them hostage? How could this have happened? They were just here no more than an hour ago. Where has he taken them?"

My disbelief turned to self-disgust when I realized that were it not for my temper-tantrum earlier, Charles would have been in that taxi and would have been able to avert this disaster.

"This is my fault -- my selfish, childish fault! Cathy and Eleanor would be safe were it not for my idiotic vanity! What do we need to do? Should we call someone?"

"I have already spoken with my commander, and he suggests that we get you to somewhere safe so that I can do some checking on my own. I have arranged for you to stay with some friends of mine on the left bank. They are very discreet and will be happy to welcome you. I suggest you pack a few things and we can get going. I will wait for you here."

Charles had withdrawn from me and our joyful giggling of less than fifteen minutes ago was buried in the enormity of what had transpired while we talked in the gardens.

"I will go with you. I will not go to your friends - Cathy is my aunt, and I got her into this, I will get her out."

"That is a courageous thought sweet Ellen, but I cannot allow it. You are in no condition to be running around Paris and will just be a distraction to me albeit a welcome one. I'll feel much better if I know that you are well looked after. You will enjoy your time with Georges and Jacqueline. They're very interesting people. She is an artist's model, and he is the artist. To be sure, they will probably feed you gossip about the art community here in Paris, but you will have such stories to take home with you when you go, and I can go about trying to figure out where your aunt is being held."

"Listen to me - I can help you. You cannot catch up to this Marco by yourself. You need someone helping you, no one will expect. Who better than me - who?"

"Mon petit Amie, as much I would like to have you with me. I cannot expose you to any more danger. Since you have been in Paris, you have been followed, knocked down, robbed and injured. You are safer with Georges and Jacqueline. I won't discuss it any further."

I took a hit of my wine, and suddenly the balcony seemed to float around me. I realized that my stomach - empty now for hours had absorbed my prescription drugs and the wine put me over the top. And unless I wanted to throw up all over my hero's shoes I better dash. I brushed past Charles, a horrified look on my face; battled with the drapes and knocked an o'jet off the table beside the French door. I just made it to the bathroom in the nick of time. Charles was pounding on the door demanding entry. He thinks I am in here crying I thought. Let him think that. I won't let him see me this way. Let him worry. He doesn't want me with him. Well, I'd show him. I would comply and go to his friends,' but if he thinks I'll stay there, he had the wrong idea.

"Ok, you're right. This is your business, not mine. I will go to stay with your friends. I'm sorry." I said meekly as I exited the bathroom. Charles appeared to be relieved to hear me say that and to see me standing on my own. Obviously, he had not been looking forward to having to pick me up off the bathroom floor and deal with my issues while he had much more urgent matters at hand.

"Are you alright? You were so ill-looking only moments ago." Just what a girl wants to hear from France's answer to James Bond, but I let it pass.

"Yes, I'm fine, only a bit of an upset stomach."

Truth be told, I was a little embarrassed about my self-induced nausea and I was grateful that no further explanation was needed.

"Let me collect a few things, and I will be ready to go. I am sure that you need as much time as you can get to try to get a head start on where this Marco is holding Cathy and Eleanor."

I withdrew from the room and went about packing a few of my things, going back into the bathroom to collect my toothbrush. I was so worried about how Cathy was faring and so sorry about being the cause of this latest disaster. I was also disappointed at missing out on what was beginning to be a promising evening and when I started to feel a tear coursing down my cheek. I gave in and laid my face in my hands and let the rest of the tears come.

I was so distraught I didn't hear the soft footfalls as Charles approached until I felt his damp arms draw me in. We didn't speak. Neither Charles nor I had any doubts about what the genesis of this latest meltdown was. We held onto each other with comfort and a trace of passion, each of us reluctant to part. After a few moments, I lifted my head and said softly, "I'm glad you're here."

Charles smiled then, a great smile full of amusement in the crinkles at the corner of his eyes and desire in the deep of them.

CHAPTER 17

After our brief but promising encounter in the loo, Charles fussed about me, helping me pull my things together. I wanted to leave some kind of note in the room for Cathy to let her know where I was in case, she found a way back from where she was being held. But Charles convinced me that the surest way to win Cathy's freedom was for me to get to somewhere safe so that he could start looking for them. He said he would let Artur the hotel manager know that we were together and certainly if Cathy knew that she wouldn't worry long. If there were any sign of her, Artur would leave a message for my dapper detective with the Sureté.

We rushed out of the hotel into a waiting taxi. Charles was guarding my every step, and in a way, I was anxious to be with his friends so that it would take some of the pressure off of him and give me an opportunity to do a little searching on my own. I knew that tomorrow night would see an end to this nightmare, but I also knew that Charles was afraid of waiting that long. I knew that he had the resources of the Sureté behind him both in manpower and technology, but I knew that he also was inclined to want to 'work alone' and I wanted to make sure that if there was anything I could be doing to help that I was doing it. I couldn't with Charles around. I hoped his friends I was to stay with weren't as watchful and protective as he was.

I was so deep in thought I didn't realize that we had pulled up in front of a patisserie and that Charles was urging me to get out of the car. I collected my things and exited the taxi. Charles stationed himself at my right shoulder as I looked around and got my bearings. We were on the left bank, obviously, because I could see the Seine on my right and the Eiffel Tower straight ahead. We were on a side street which was quite busy even at this time of night. People were strolling along laughing. Some groups were sitting at the outside tables in front of a neighborhood cafe talking quietly and smoking - every once in a while, erupting into laughter -- I was overwhelmed by the charm of this place. I was only sorry that I hadn't been paying attention in the cab on the way here. I would have then known how to find my way out. I tried to see the street signs, but it was too dark, and the only thing I could make out was the glow of the lights along the Seine.

Charles ushered me along into the building in front of us. The entrance was to the left of the door to the patisserie. The doors to the apartment must have been ten feet high and easily four feet wide each. Beside the doors were mailboxes and a buzzer marked "Luniere." It was the only buzzer, leading me to the conclusion that the friends Charles was entrusting my babysitting to were Jacqueline and George Luniere.

Charles buzzed us, and from above we could hear the scrape of a chair moving over the floor, muted footsteps and an answering buzz to admit us.

At the top of a narrow stairwell in the glow of a wall sconce stood the most beautiful woman I had ever seen. She was at least 5' 8", red-headed and with skin which could only be described as cream. She was smiling openly with no hint of the French hauteur, her green eyes wide and twinkling. Clearly, she was fond of Charles - *how fond I wondered*? There would be no chance for a wounded 5' 1" slightly lumpy Americaine in the battle for the heart of this cop. I hoped she was married and very devoted to Georges.

Jacqueline took me in close to her and told me how 'glad she was to meet me,' blah blah 'sorry about the trouble I had had in Paris so far' and yada yada 'sure Charles would have my Aunt and Eleanor back to me before I could say Fromage!

There was absolutely no way I was going to avoid liking her, so I had better get planning.

Charles was muttering en Francais with Georges, and it was beyond my powers of interpretation to discern if he was instructing his friend to keep me locked up with bread and water or if they were discussing the chances of the French soccer team in the upcoming season. I'd like to think it was the latter, but in all likelihood, it wasn't. I hoped that Georges and Jacqueline would be too busy posing for each other to keep an eye on little old me. I wanted to blend in with the wallpaper so that I had a chance to slip away.

"Well, ma petit, I must leave you. Georges and Jacqueline will keep you entertained, and

I hope out of trouble while I am gone. When I return, I will have your aunt and her Amie with me. Be good." He kissed me lightly on the lips and embraced me just a little too firmly. I could sense his reluctance to leave me, probably knowing I would try to outwit his friends.

"Please let me come with you, Charles. I will do whatever you tell me to, and I would be much more helpful than the corp of detectives you plan to have accompany you. They don't know what Cathy looks like -- I do! Please?"

"Non, and that is, as they say, final! Au revoir." With that and a pat on the head, he was gone.

"You must be famished. Let me get you something to eat!" Jacqueline said.

"Oh, I'd love to eat at that cafe downstairs. Wouldn't it be nice? We could watch the people go by. I haven't sat in a cafe in the whole time I've been here. What do you say?"

"I definitely do not think that that would be a good idea. You are obviously a target of some kind and Charles would never forgive us if anything happened to you."

This from Georges, who, despite his occupation, was built like a career Marine.

"How dangerous can it be - - it's night-time! If we sit in the shadows, no one will even see us. How about it?"

"Non, perhaps in the morning. For now, I will fix you some eggs - perhaps an omelet - and I have some nice crusty rolls."

"Yes, that will be nice. Merci." I gave in. I was too tired to escape tonight anyway. I would go in the morning before my pleasant captors awoke. A good sleep would probably be the best idea.

After a marvelous omelet and the promised rolls - and an aperitif I really didn't need, Jacqueline made up a bed for me in the studio. As I lay awake with the faint but not unpleasant odor of the oils in the air, I tried to imagine where Cathy and Eleanor could be. And then in a bolt just before I drifted off, it came to me -- I didn't know where they were now, but I had a pretty good idea where they would be tomorrow night about 2 am.

CHAPTER 18

The first thing that Charles had to do was to let the other ladies in the party know that Cathy, Eleanor, and Ellen would be staying on in France and that they must leave. He didn't want to alarm them, but they were just more potential hostages, and he felt the great need to get them out of the country before they too disappeared.

He drove to the Tour d'Argent restaurant where he had made reservations for the whole party. Even though more than 2 hours had passed since they had left for the restaurant,

Charles was fairly sure they would still be there. French dining very often was an evening-long event, and at the grand Tour d'Argent, the sumptuous dinner could still be underway.

He stopped his car out front, and the valet approached to take it away.

"Non! I will be needing this shortly" he explained while simultaneously flipping his id in the valet's face. "Please call a cab immediately. Some of your patrons will be coming out in a few minutes. I do not want them kept waiting."

Charles realized that he was being abrupt with the valet, but he was in a rush and had shifted into his cop persona. The gallant and amenable Frenchman had disappeared with one phone call from Marco.

Charles felt very guilty that his investigation had put this nice group of older women in danger and terrified that things could get worse! Despite his comments to Ellen about how rarely art investigations became dangerous, Charles was worried about this one. Marco had been out of sight for 10 years – what had caused him to come forward now?

Charles entered the restaurant and saw the group seated in a banquette toward the back.

The group was quiet, but as they saw him approach, they became more animated.

"Inspector Blanchard! Where have you been – you've entirely missed the meal!" exclaimed Jessica. "And where are Cathy, Ellen, and Eleanor? Oh, I hope nothing has gone wrong!"

"Well, as a matter of fact, my dear ladies, I am afraid we will have to go. There has been a bit of an emergency which I will tell you about after we return to the hotel."

Charles did not want to frighten them, but he knew that he would have to tell them enough of the truth to relieve their concern without scaring them.

Susan stood up and announced that in that case, they should get going. While Charles took care of the bill, the five women quickly pulled their belongings together and got ready to leave. Vivian always the last to be ready for anything was attempting to finish her aperitif and was solely responsible for the first declarative statement the ladies had heard from Laura on the trip.

"For goodness sake, Vivian, how can you finish that drink? Didn't you hear from the inspector that there has been an emergency? We need to go!"

Vivian equally surprised at Laura's outburst as the other ladies, complied uncharacteristically easily and gathered her belongings as well.

Charles packed the now bustling ladies in the cab and followed behind in his vehicle. At the front of the hotel, he herded them up to Cathy and Ellen's suite and sat them down to explain.

The five women arranged themselves throughout the room occasionally glancing around as if Ellen and Cathy would appear with Eleanor at any moment.

"What IS going on, Inspector?" Susan as the defacto leader of the group tried to hide her worry about their missing friends.

"Well, as you know I have been involved in a case of sorts since before I met all of you. When I crossed paths with you at the D'Orsay Museum, I was there looking for information and inspiration." Charles drew a deep breath before continuing.

"Unfortunately, a criminal has taken this situation to another level and has threatened your friends because of your association with me. I am very sorry that this has involved you and so I think it is necessary for you to leave for England a day early. Cathy, Eleanor, and Ellen will follow in a day or two, but I have had to seclude them. They are safe of course, but I think it would be best if you went on ahead without them."

The ladies wore stunned expressions – *what had happened*?

Vivian spoke first. "Well, sir, I totally appreciate your concern for us, but there are certain elements of our itinerary which we haven't completed. And I shouldn't like to leave without seeing Paris from the Seine or without going to Giverny."

Charles could almost hear Scarlett O'Hara herself 'fiddle-dee-dee!' in Vivian's tone, but his brooked no argument.

"Madame, I am sorry you are disappointed to have missed seeing those things, but perhaps you can come back again someday. I don't feel that you are safe here. Do you understand that?" He spoke more pointedly than he wanted to, but he felt it was imperative that the women realize how much danger they were in.

"Susan, what do you think?" Laura asked. Since her outburst at the restaurant, Laura had been quiet. But clearly, she was now getting scared.

"I think that the Inspector wouldn't have gone to the lengths he has if he didn't feel it was important. I shall be sorry to miss our trip to Giverny, but perhaps with the extra day in

England, we can arrange something else we hadn't been planning to do. Like, taking Vivian to the Tower of London, for instance." Susan said with a laugh.

She was well aware that these women were depending on her to set the right tone and the tone right now required calm and compromise.

CHAPTER 19

I slept late.

When I awoke, the studio was bright with sunlight. I could hear low murmurs in the rooms outside.

I shook my head. I must really have overdone it on the alcohol and painkillers last night, I thought to myself. As for pain - well there was that - as a matter of fact, a great deal of pain. But a more pressing problem emerged as I assessed myself. My sling had slipped off during the night, and my shoulder felt as if it had dislocated again.

I had trouble getting myself upright and as I rolled to the side to lever myself up a great bolt of pain shot up my arm - the suddenness and acuteness of it brought a scream to my lips and tears to my eyes.

"What is it - what has happened?" Georges was in the room before the nausea reached my head.

"I am afraid my little tumble in the fountain last night caused my sling to loosen overnight. I'm afraid that I may have dislocated my shoulder again." Just then another star-spangled jolt struck me, and I passed out.

This time when I awoke, I found myself in the back of a Parisian ambulance. Again.

At the hospital this time, I was treated by a very kind doctor - a woman determined that I was going to recuperate there. For at least overnight. My arm was a mess she declared. I had definitely not followed doctor's orders, and I was going to have to take it easy, where an experienced medical eye could be kept on me. Then she came at me with a syringe - Demerol I hoped.

When the Demerol wore off, it was nighttime. I noticed that my room faced the

Seine and I wondered if I could see it - the d'Orsay. I got somewhat unsteadily out of bed and went to the window and leaned on the sill. The moon was bright over the Seine, and I could just make it out. The translucent dome was dark. I wondered what time it was. I went to the bed table and looked for my watch - *1:30 am. Perhaps I still had time.*

Quickly, I gathered my things together and dressed swiftly. Unfortunately, Jacqueline and George had had me transported in only the sleeveless nightgown I wore to bed. I couldn't very well go anywhere in that nightie, and the hospital had not equipped me with pants this time. *What was I going to do?* Then I noticed that there was another bed in my room and the twenty-something with her leg in traction didn't seem to be going anywhere.

Perhaps she had some clothes with her. I dug through the other closet, and I found a sweatshirt, some jogging shorts, and hospital slippers. I would have to forego a bra. Fortunately, the shorts were spandex, and while not the size I would choose for myself, they would do in a pinch. I squeezed myself into my borrowed clothes and quietly slipped from the room after checking the hallway. All was quiet, and I tiptoed down to the door marked as an exit.

Once out on the street I quickly made for the bridge. The Seine was still active even at this hour. The boats glided softly along, making only the slightest of ripples on the surface.

I could see the d'Orsay from here, and I knew that somewhere in the shadows, the cretin who was responsible for kidnapping Cathy and Eleanor (and for tearing Charles away from me), lurked.

I was nervous. I had never been the adventurous sort, and I was pretty sure, racing through the streets leading to the bridge I had my eye on, was probably not on Fodor's list of recommended walks in Paris. Well, chances were that either I would be accosted here, or accosted by the kidnapper in the d'Orsay, so I decided I might as well die trying to get Cathy back, and that meant I had better get to the museum.

In a relatively short amount of time, I found myself at the outside edge of the museum building. I stopped to take a breath and make a plan. I spent a moment or two formulating an impractical plan -- I wasn't really in any shape to scale the bricks and outcroppings of the building, and I was pretty sure that I didn't have my cat-burglar-glass-cutting equipment with me, so as a last resort I did what under normal circumstances would not work.   I tried the front door. Unbelievably, it was unlocked.

CHAPTER 20

Once inside my momentary bravery deserted me. Despite the fact that I had entered through an unlocked door, I was pretty sure I shouldn't be here. But now that I was, I may as well see if the gallant Msr. Blanchard was.

I wondered if the fact that the door was unlocked meant that the alarm systems were disabled as well. I was shocked that the door was not locked. And the fact that it was, set me to worry that before very long I would run into the full power of the Sureté. My instincts told me that they surely wouldn't go off leaving a museum loaded with priceless artwork un-guarded.

My instincts were excellent. I left the foyer and entered into the main museum area. The museum itself was in relative darkness. There were emergency lights on here and there but no display lighting. I headed for the stairs to the right. These stairs would lead me to the gallery where I had first met Charles. As I entered the gallery itself, I heard a footfall, and before I could react, a hand was covering my mouth, and I was dragged behind a short partition. I struggled of course, but my jailer was much stronger and had two strong arms. Suddenly, I was spun around, and I was facing Det. Lt. Boutin.

He motioned for me not to speak. I nodded my assent, and he whispered: "I won't even inquire why you are here, but now that you are you will be silent." He handcuffed me by my good hand to his left one and proceeded to tug me along behind him. I mutely followed him, and after a time he stopped stock still and pointed ahead of him.

There was a shadow moving in front of the giant clock.

Even though the shadow appeared to be stooping, it seemed to be a tall man, very slim and with an elongated head. My captor motioned me to remain silent. I was frozen in fear anyway, so I capitulated without a second thought.

We stayed very still for a moment, and I wondered what Boutin was planning. Would he just watch for a few moments, or would he spring upon his prey? At that thought, I wondered what he would do with me. I was bonded to him with his own handcuffs, and I speculated that if he chose to pounce on the shadow, that I would provide the coup d' grace. Two for the price of one.

The same thought must have occurred to the good detective, and he raised our linked arms in a gesture of 'Like, see what you've done now? I can't take down the bad guy 'cuz I have to drag you around.' As we were both pondering the next move, I noticed that the shadow seemed to be moving toward us. He had something in his hand beside him, and I figured we would soon find out what our next move would be. We didn't have long to wait.

The figure made a sudden move toward us (or perhaps to the exit behind us), and my reluctant bodyguard screamed

"Arrete!" *as in I'm not going to ask nicely, just freeze!.*

Apparently, French thugs didn't respond well to reason as he continued toward us undeterred by the authority of Boutin's voice. I had compromised the situation, and I knew that it was up to me to make up for it, so I quickly kicked out my left leg, just in time to connect with his oncoming form. As I have indicated before, I am neither small nor large, but my surprise move was well-timed enough to bring the big guy to the floor of the D'Orsay, in a touching fetal position, the gun he had been holding skittering across the floor. The felon's free-fall, however, created a chain reaction which resulted in a 'pig pile on the prisoner.' Boutin, fortuitously for the mission (not so much for me), landed on top of me and was able to remove the cap on our fallen prey and reveal his identity.

As I had noticed before, the man was tall, and his face was long – not one of Mother Nature's finest specimens, but definitely European in ancestry. He had a familiar look to him – one that I couldn't place right now while laying on top of him handcuffed to a very mad French policeman who was struggling to get off of me, but something struck me about him.

At that moment, a number of things happened – not the least of which was that the perp started to struggle. Perhaps it was the weight of one American woman added to the weight of one French Policeman, but the struggle was in vain.

The criminal stopped struggling long enough to utter something in French which may or may not have been "Arrest me already, but please get off of me you're killing me!" And at the same time, I heard a chuckle emanate not from above me or underneath me but from across the room, and I angled my head up to see my favorite Frenchman standing across from us his rarely used gun aimed at the bottom of the pile.

"I'll give you this mademoiselle, you never cease to amaze and frighten me!" Charles said with a glimmer of respect, fear, and warmth in his voice.

"Now, let's see about getting you all up on your feet." Charles had his gun still trained on the man beneath me which apparently gave Boutin the confidence to get up and help me up. The prisoner we left on the floor, breathing deeply.

CHAPTER 21

Eleanor and Cathy were just as surprised as Ellen and Charles when their escort to the restaurant turned out to be their captor. Instead of taking them to a restaurant, he continued to drive around Paris and its suburbs until the wee hours of the morning. It was almost as if he were waiting for instructions on where to take them. They had heard crackling radio transmissions in French, but with their limited knowledge of the language they couldn't make out the conversation.

After a few hours, the man made a cell phone call – also muttered in French and then he stopped the cab next to a red Renault sedan, produced a gun and ordered them out of the cab on a dark, deserted street on the outskirts of Paris. The driver of the Renault manhandled them into the back of the car, and their driver got into the front passenger seat.

Then things got frightening. The driver and the passenger fumbled in the front seat with something and turned around to face them with gas masks over their faces. The passenger produced a spray bottle, and with 2 squirts on it, everything for Eleanor and Cathy went black.

When they awoke, they were tied together on a soft mattress. They were blindfolded and Cathy had a lingering headache. Their mouths were neatly taped with duct tape. But they were warm and despite their bindings, comfortable.

She was instantly concerned about Eleanor – she was much older, and Cathy was concerned that she would suffer from the gas attack or from being gagged. Then she felt a struggle beside her and realized that Eleanor was at least, alive.

Eleanor was spitting mad! *Where were they – how dare that scruffy young man do this to them? Where were the others – were they ok? Was Cathy ok?* She hadn't felt any movement beside her, but she felt someone beside her, and most likely it was Cathy.

At that moment, she began to struggle with the ropes binding her, and she felt the person beside her struggle as well.

"Ellllllleanor" she heard "umph" she replied, realizing that this was indeed Cathy.

The two women worked side by side on their bindings. Cathy's began to loosen, and she was just able to slide a thumb and a forefinger on her right hand out. She used these to pick and pick at the knots on her left hand. For ten or fifteen minutes she struggled, occasionally stopping to catch her breath. At last the left hand was freed, and the right hand followed.

The first thing she did was to remove the tape over her mouth and then the blindfold over her eyes. Then she turned her attention to Eleanor. She removed the tape over Eleanor's mouth first, and Eleanor gasped for air first then yelled; "God-dammit! Cathy, is that really you? How dare they do this to us! When I find that stinking little Frenchman, I'll subject him to this same punishment!"

By this time Eleanor's blindfold had been removed, and Cathy was freeing her hands. Once that was done, the two of them worked on releasing the ropes trapping their ankles.

"Free!" Cathy exulted.

The two of them looked around the room and realized instantly, that they were in some kind of storage room. There was no window, and a quick inspection of the large oak door revealed no door handle. The stone walls made for a cool, damp atmosphere and the one light bulb in the room cast an eerie pall over their quarters.

There was no outside noise – no blaring horns – no rushing feet. And there was no way for them to tell if it was morning or night.

"I don't suppose there is a bathroom," Eleanor said a bit urgently.

"Well, let's get up and explore – perhaps there is something behind one of those shelves," Cathy suggested.

Eleanor stood up gingerly. The hours spent tied up had caused her calves to stiffen up, and Cathy was noticing the same thing. After a moment the two felt limber enough to set out exploring their prison.

Lucky enough for them behind the last shelf was a door and on the other side of that door which fortunately was unlocked was a small bathroom – with a window! The window seemed to be at or below street level, so the only view was the occasional well-shod foot.

Eleanor was the first to take advantage of the facilities, and while she waited for her friend, Cathy looked around. The first thing she noticed was that the room was storing rack upon rack of toilet paper, boxes of soap bars, canned goods, and other provisions.

"Huh!" Cathy shouted, causing Eleanor who was emerging from the lavatory to comment "What, what is it?"

"Look at this Eleanor – this soap says, 'Courtesy of the Hotel St. Jeanne". That's our hotel! Could we be in the basement?"

"This is unbelievable! Those cretins drive us all around Paris for hours, drug us, only to basically leave us where we started from!" Eleanor was stupefied.

"Well, think of it this way, Cathy suggested – We weren't hurt, and once we get ourselves out of here we will not have far to go to get to our rooms and shower!" "Now, let's find a way out of here!"

The two women prowled the room looking for any other sign of an exit, but with the exception of the small window in the bathroom, there was no other way to imagine escaping.

"Chances are this storeroom isn't used very often, otherwise why would they put us here?" Eleanor commented.

"Yes, but they may have made one mistake! They either forgot or disregarded the fact that there's a window in that bathroom. We can use that!" said Cathy, clearly plotting something.

"You don't mean one of us is going to try to get out? There is no room!", Eleanor exclaimed.

"No, I know we can't fit out the window, but we can use it to draw attention to us. It must already be early morning, traffic will be picking up, and I bet if we can put up a sign or something, before long someone will notice." Cathy explained.

"I have a better idea – let's break the window and find something to toss out there. I know people don't often look down where they walk, but if something bright catches their eye as they approach, they may stop!" Eleanor was suddenly enthusiastic about this plan.

At that moment the door to the storage room started to rattle. Both women quickly and quietly closed the bathroom door and resumed their positions on the bed. After a moment they heard a bolt slide back.

They closed their eyes and hoped that their captor would not notice that their bindings were removed. Fortunately, the light was in the center of the room, and their mattress was in a dark corner. Cathy, who was facing the door managed a quick peek from her lightly closed eyes and saw their taxi driver from the night before, peer around the partially open door. Satisfied with what he saw, he withdrew and slid the bolt across.

After fifteen or twenty minutes the two heard the bolt slide again. They pretended to be stirring, figuring that their captor would not still expect them to be out cold. They'd wisely used the intervening time to tie their legs together loosely. They decided their captor would expect them to have tried to escape their binds and it wouldn't be so bad if their hands were untied and their blindfolds and gags removed. The worst that could happen is that he would bind them again. This time Cathy had secreted a sharp piece of metal under the pillow to aid them in removing them again if they had to.

This time the captor came into the room and placed a tray on the floor and came over to the bed. "Ah, so you ladies have been busy, no? D'accord. It is alright. I am about to free you so you can eat!" The man was not so menacing as the night before, and he set about removing the rest of the bindings.

"I am sorry you had to be tied up so long. We don't want you hurt – we will only keep you here as long as we need to. Marco is no monster." At that, the last of the binding was removed, and the man moved over to the tray and placed it on the bed.

"Do you realize that we are two old ladies and that we could easily have a heart attack or develop a clot being bound all this time," Cathy cried.

"Yes, Madame I do, that is why I will check on you for as long as you need, and I will make sure you are ok. How about a stroll around the room every ½ hour to stretch your legs?

"Generous of you. What is your name young man?" Eleanor drawled.

"I am called Albert."

Cathy and Eleanor ate as instructed, but as soon as they finished, Albert ushered them to the bathroom. And when they finished, bound their hands again and set them gently on the bed.

"Au Revoir, Mesdames, I will check on you again in a bit. In the meantime, please behave". With that, he withdrew, and the bolt slid into place again, leaving their lightly eaten food tray behind.

Cathy and Eleanor leaned back and pretended to relax while Albert exited.

"Cathy, let's just stay here for a little while – make sure he doesn't come back!" Eleanor whispered. "Ok." Cathy agreed with Eleanor.

After a few minutes, they became sleepy and began to nod off. As she drifted slowly to sleep, Cathy realized that their food must have been drugged.

When Cathy woke again, it was dark in the room. She had no way of knowing whether it was day or night. She realized that she and Eleanor needed to get ready to put their plan into action.

"Eleanor – Eleanorrrrr, pssst wake up!" Cathy whispered. Eleanor began to stir and, in a moment opened her eyes.

"We need to get out of here Eleanor – now! I don't know when Albert made his last check on us, so we need to move!"

Eleanor was tired and stiff and worried about getting caught. Her usual spunk had deserted her hours ago when they were tied up again.

"But we should wait don't you think until his next check to know how long before he comes back?" Eleanor reasoned.

"Yes, I agree, but then we need to be ready to go....I really don't believe that if he were going to check on us every ½ hour, he would have drugged us, so he is probably not going to check again until dinner time, but we have to be ready to leave. Let's at least see if we can get to the bathroom and determine if it is day or night." Cathy urged.

After about 5 or so minutes the two ladies had managed to free themselves again and decided that one of them would check the window in the bathroom. The other would look around for something that would do for a weapon in case Albert returned, and something to catch the attention of a passerby, should they manage to escape.

They peered around the room and looked on the shelves for something brightly colored that would attract attention but found nothing. And then, ironically, it was their captor that provided the perfect object. A cardinal red linen napkin left on the food tray!

"This napkin is precisely what we needed!" Cathy exulted.

The news from the bathroom wasn't good. It was dark out, and there seemed to be no foot traffic around – so no hope of getting someone's attention. Cathy quietly closed the bathroom door behind her and went looking for Eleanor who was searching out a weapon.

There was nothing that screamed weapon until Cathy tripped across something on the floor -- a large urn – apparently from some prior flower arrangement. The container was heavy but, in a pinch, could be used to bash their captor over the head.

She and Eleanor made their way back to the bed to think of another plan. No sooner had they settled, there was a noise at the door. Unfortunately for them the urn/weapon was still back in the corner where they found it. Quickly they settled back on the bed but with eyes open and focused on the door. This time a large grey-haired man opened the door, not the malleable Albert.

"Ah, ladies, I am sure you were expecting Albert, but I am very sorry – I am the second shift! Now, I have some dinner for you. Sorry, it is so late. I figured you would probably be still sleeping. If you are wondering if I had your food drugged again, I did not. There is nothing you can accomplish at this time of night, and besides, soon you will be free! Once Charles Blanchard complies with my demands, I will have you released. After I am safely away that is. Now, eat your dinner. I had some tea brewed for you. I thought that you might be chilled in this drafty cellar."

"What do you want with Charles?" Cathy demanded as she sized up their latest captor and clearly the leader of the group who had kidnapped them. He was a tall man, older and grey-haired, but possessing a lithe body.

Someone she might have been attracted to had he not kidnapped, gassed and drugged her first.

Clearly, he was well-born. His clothes were impeccable, and his mannerisms were refined. "Where do you come from and what is your name?" Cathy asked.

"You may call me Marco, and I think it would be best if I didn't tell you any more about myself."

Eleanor quiet during Cathy's questioning had something to say herself.

"You seem like a man who would not treat two old ladies like this. Let us go, and since we don't know anything about you, we won't be able to tell the police anything useful!"

"Non, Madam, I cannot. Not until I get what I need. Then, I assure you, you will be safe."

With that, he walked to the corner of the room and unfolded a table and two chairs and dressed the table. After the food was placed on it, he invited the women to sit.

"I am sure you are sick of that mattress. Please sit here and enjoy a civilized meal. I have had it prepared at a nearby restaurant, and I am sure you will enjoy it. Yes, I know that you have removed your bindings, but I really don't think they are necessary now that we are so close to the end."

With that Cathy and Eleanor stood up and came to the table on which was a lovely mouthwatering meal. Glistening duck, creamy potatoes and asparagus that looked like it had just left the pan. Marco poured each of them a cup of aromatic tea and then said. "I will leave you to enjoy your meal. Bon Appetit!" At that, he withdrew from the room leaving its occupants stunned and starving. They tucked into their meal realizing how hungry they were, and each enjoyed two more precious cups of tea.

After eating they went and sat on the bed to plan their next move. Their legs and heads were heavy from the meal and before long they began to doze.

Marco had lied. Well, not exactly. He told them he hadn't drugged their meal, but he had laced the tea with a mild sedative. Neither lady was going anywhere tonight.

CHAPTER 22

After seeing to it that the prisoner was handcuffed (Boutin kindly removed the cuffs from me and placed them on him), and led away. Charles got down to the heart of the matter – who the man was, what I was doing there, where did I get the clothes I was wearing and finally – was I all right?

I tried to answer the questions, with as much dignity as a woman wearing too-tight spandex shorts and who is braless, could.

"Charles, I know I told you I would stay out of this, but I woke up in the hospital and knew exactly where he would be and since I got my Aunt involved in this, I wanted to make sure we got him... I got these clothes from a woman who was in my room in the hospital – her leg was broken, so she wasn't using them..."

"The hospital!" he roared – what were you doing at the hospital? Last time I saw you, you were at Georges and Jacqueline's – how did you end up there?"

"Charles, I know you're mad, but can we not do this here? My arm is really sore and how can I say this delicately, I have to go to the bathroom. Can we just get out of here?" Charles nodded his assent and ushered me to the door. As we stepped outside, I waited while he spoke with one of the cops *probably reminding him to lock up the D'Orsay before he left*, I mused.

We went back to the hotel, and this time Charles had a policeman follow us to the room. He sent me to the bathroom and asked the young cop to wait outside in the hallway.

When I returned from the bathroom, I could tell that Charles was anxious to finally have me answer the questions that I had temporarily avoided answering. He was still steaming, and I wondered if his mood would improve once I answered....I was about to find out.

"So, I have spoken to Georges, and he told me that you passed out at their apartment after your sling fell apart and that you were taken to the hospital to stay overnight because your shoulder dislocated AGAIN! Exactly who told you, you could leave?"

"I told you, I woke up in the hospital and realized that I knew where Marco would be and so I decided I needed to be here --- did he tell you where my Aunt and Eleanor are?"

"No, he did not, primarily because he is not Marco," Charles said

"He isn't Marco? Who is he?" I said astonished.

"Probably one of Marco's henchmen. I saw the same clue as you did '2am - Mardi - D'O.'. But I think it was intended to lead us away from what was really happening – something that I am going to now try to piece together. You will stay here – and to make sure I have posted an officer outside your room. I should not have put the responsibility on Georges and Jacqueline – not for keeping you out of trouble. That job clearly is something best left to the police."

"Charles, let me come with you – I know that I'm a liability, but I'm sure I could help –

Cathy is my Aunt, and I am ultimately the one who is responsible for her kidnapping!" I begged.

"No, if I have to worry about where you are and if you are in danger, I won't be able to do what I have to do. You will stay here. I will call you when I can to let you know what is going on." His voice softened. "You need to get some rest. In all likelihood, the man we have in custody will be able to give us clues, but I'm going to have to interrogate him, and I don't need you for that."

"I could offer to sit on him again – maybe then he will spill his guts!" I joked. "Please Charles!"

"Non. I will call you. Now get into that bed and rest, and please, go easy on my officer outside."

With that Charles kissed me on the forehead and left the room. I heard him speak with the guard outside and then – silence.

CHAPTER 23

I'm not usually a schemer but after Charles left me I sat, and I plotted elaborate ways that I could distract the cop at my door so that I could go and help Charles. But none of my elaborate plans could get me past the fact that I was in a strange city with no idea where Charles was going, and I didn't want to delay his finding Aunt Cathy and Eleanor because he was looking for me. So, I resolved to do as he asked and wait in the room to hear from him.

I changed into a loose t-shirt, took a pain pill and got into bed even though it was nearly dawn. But I couldn't sleep; I kept thinking of Cathy and Eleanor and worrying about what was happening to them. 'Who was the man at the museum? Why did he look so familiar? Where was Marco?' Before long I was starting to get drowsy.

When I woke, it was bright outside, and the clock read Noon. "Noon! My God! How could I have slept so long?" I wondered if Charles had reported into the guard out front, so I walked out to the door of the suite, passing through the sitting room on my way. I reflected on how lucky we had been to be given the suite after the break-in when it hit me – the man in the museum was none other than our Hotel Detective! That's how the room was ransacked – and he presumably was my mugger the 2nd day I was here!

I pulled open the door to announce it to the cop outside, only to find my door unguarded.

I rushed back into the room and quickly bolted and chained the door. 'Where was the guard?' Over the next hour, I checked numerous times, and the guard never came back. *Even if he'd snuck out to the bathroom or to grab a smoke, he should have come back by now*, I mused.

I was becoming apprehensive – after days of being under guard by my Aunt, Charles, Georges and Jacqueline and now the cop, I was suddenly alone and feeling very vulnerable.

CHAPTER 24

Charles had realized immediately that the man at the museum was the hotel detective. He knew the moment he looked at the handcuffed man. He didn't tell Ellen, however, because he knew what her reaction would be and now, he just needed her safe and in one place.

He returned her to the hotel and put one of his men at the door. George Bertrand was an experienced officer and a family man. He had worked alongside Charles for more than 10 years, and Charles trusted him. He knew that if he had George at the door, there would be no fear that anything could happen to Ellen. Of course, Ellen would try to scheme her way out of the room, but Charles was confident that, despite being a Frenchman, George would be able to resist her.

After leaving the Hotel St. Jeanne, Charles returned to the d'Orsay Museum. His team was beginning to pack up but stopped what they were doing when they saw Charles. He would want to look around himself. Charles could always be counted on to find that crucial piece of evidence that blew open the case -- at least for the past 10 years. That one failure with the Hassam 10 years ago had made Charles into a perfectionist. Every crime scene was scrubbed twice – once by the evidence team and once by Charles. It wasn't that he didn't trust his team, but he wouldn't have been satisfied unless he looked himself.

Charles addressed the matter at hand and began his painstaking search throughout the museum exhibit halls. It wasn't enough to search the one where they had caught the decoy – and that is just what Charles thought the hotel detective was – a decoy. He must go through each exhibit and make sure that nothing else was missing or disturbed.

He was also confused. Marco had told him that the exchange would take place at the D'Orsay that night. Not only had Marco not shown but the Hotel Dick had been captured instead, and it seemed as if the painting in question hadn't been touched. He hadn't heard from Marco since and so now Charles was wondering why this man who had prompted his presence at the D'Orsay, had been a no-show.

Merde! So close and yet so far! Charles concluded that the Hotel Detective must have been there at the orders of Marco and perhaps since Boutin and Ellen took him down he didn't have a chance to make a switch. But he didn't have the other painting on him when he was arrested so where was it? Was the Hotel Detective pulling a fast one or did Marco get greedy?

Charles realized that he was not going to get anywhere by wondering, so he took one more glance at the Renoir painting that Marco was so interested in, deciding to leave the tracking device in place when he noticed a small gap at the edge of the frame.....

The canvas was missing here, and then he realized that the remaining edge of the was pulling up. A closer look revealed, not the aged canvas he had expected, but a newer, thicker fabric. This painting was not the original! Somehow, Marco had managed the switch, leaving a copy in place of the original and even reattaching the GPS, to appear as if the painting was undisturbed. Now Charles understood why the Hotel Detective was there – as a distraction!

And now Marco was in possession of two precious works of art. And, Charles had failed twice.

CHAPTER 25

When Cathy and Eleanor woke again, they got to their feet gingerly and quietly in case Albert or Marco was outside the door. Then, almost on tiptoes, they made their way to the back of the room where the bathroom was located.

In the light from the bathroom window, Cathy was able to read her watch. 1 p.m.! They had slept since the night before! A glance out the window confirmed it was daylight.

"Now let's find a way to break the glass, quietly!" Cathy whispered.

The window was slightly too high for Cathy to reach, but Eleanor was a head taller, and her arms seemed to reach the window comfortably. Traffic appeared to be picking up on the sidewalk outside. French men and women on their way to lunch – with perhaps a quick side trip to the zinc bar for a quick shot of Calvados.

She pushed at the glass, hoping that there would be a loose spot. And there was. The grout in the lower left corner was beginning to decay, and after ten or so minutes, Eleanor was able to scrape enough away to loosen the left side of the pane.

Cathy busied herself looking for a piece of wood or metal to use as a pry bar and finally found an old piece of iron that looked like it had once been part of a railing. She scraped it against the stone walls and floor to sharpen the end. After a few minutes, she brought it to Eleanor, but it wasn't needed, Eleanor had removed all but one small corner of the grout, and the small glass pane toppled out onto the sidewalk.

The tinkling of the glass was noticed immediately by someone wearing bright red high heel pumps. And she stopped a moment, long enough to see a hastily waved red napkin and to hear HELP!

****

The lovely Frenchwoman who noticed them had quickly notified the manager at the hotel, wondering why they were keeping their guests, prisoner in the basement. The manager himself unlocked the door and ushered Cathy and Eleanor to safety.

"Mesdames, my abject apologies. I cannot imagine how you came to be locked in the storeroom." Cathy quickly interjected that they woke up in there after a harrowing kidnapping and showed them the duct tape and rope as evidence. The manager's face fell as their story unfolded and immediately called for the hotel security guard.

"We will talk with him after we shower and get a cup of coffee into us," Eleanor said firmly. With that, she and Cathy, accompanied by the Frenchwoman and the hotel manager exited the basement. Cathy nervously looked around, half expecting their captor to show up around the corner.

The manager showed them to Cathy's room with a flourish and had already ordered that hot coffee and croissants be delivered. He told them he would be back in an hour with security to get their story, then he left them alone after another lengthy apology.

Ellen was not in the room, which Cathy found strange and she wondered if she were with Charles.

"The first thing I am going to do is call Inspector Blanchard, Ellen must be with him – why wouldn't she be here? I also want him here when the hotel detective arrives. I don't trust these rent-a-cops, and I have to wonder if our abduction was related to the attack on Ellen and the ransacking of our room!" Cathy said in frustration.

"An excellent idea, Cathy. Although I imagine that Ellen is fine. But I do agree that Charles should be called. I am going to take a shower and will be back in half an hour. Keep the coffee hot!" With that Eleanor left the room.

Cathy looked around a bit but didn't find any clue to Ellen's whereabouts. She was dialing the phone when the doorknob rattled, and after a moment during which Cathy picked up her shoe to use as a weapon, Ellen appeared in the doorway.

"Cathy! Where have you been? Charles is out combing Paris for you!" I exclaimed!

"Ellen – are you all right? I've been worried since I came back and found the room empty." Cathy cried at about the same time.

I rushed to her side, so relieved at last that Cathy was safe, and we shared a long hug. "But what about Eleanor – is she here?"

"No sweetie she's taking a shower in her room. I defy anyone to mess with her again. Eleanor might be in her 70s, but she is tough!"

"Well, I'm fine too, although I am surprised about that. Charles brought me back here last night after an – erm – incident at the d'Orsay Museum and posted a policeman at the door. When I woke up this morning the cop was gone. I worried that that meant someone was going to break in and attack me, so I quickly dressed and left the room. I have been down in the restaurant ever since. I decided that I needed to be somewhere with lots of people around. But what I want to know is what happened to you?"

Before I tell you, I want to contact the police. Inspector Blanchard should know we have returned, and I don't think we should wait for the Hotel Detective.

"Well you'd be waiting for some time for him," I explained. "He is currently cooling his heels at the police station. The situation at the d'Orsay involved him – actually it involved me tripping and then falling on top of him, which conveniently allowed Charles to capture him!"

I had much to tell my aunt and, from the looks of Cathy, she had, had quite a few days as well. Cathy was right. "Yes, we need Charles here now!" I agreed.

"He will be relieved to know that you are safely back but also, perhaps he can tell us if we are safe here. Since the Hotel Detective is involved in the case, I am not sure we can trust this hotel staff!"

Cathy was again dialing the police station, and I quietly waited for the call to go through.

Cathy asked for Inspector Blanchard and was told he would have to call her back. He did so in less than a minute. I answered the phone and blurted out "Charles, I am at the hotel, and Cathy and Eleanor are here – I don't quite know what happened to them, but we need to see you before the Hotel Manager returns with security."

I didn't have to wait long for Charles response -

"Bon. I will be there in 20 minutes. Don't let anyone in and don't talk with anyone until I get there. Au Revoir." With that, the connection ended.

Cathy and I spent 5 or 10 minutes freshening up, and as we were finishing up, there was a knock on the door.

"Well, that was fast!" Cathy said. She went to the door and opened it enough to see that it was a refreshed looking Eleanor chomping at the bit to get some answers.

Cathy let Eleanor in and was just filling her in on her call to Blanchard when there was another knock on the door. Expecting now that it was the inspector, she hastily pulled open the door only to find Albert from the night before standing there with a gun.

CHAPTER 26

C harles left Boutin in charge of continuing the so far useless interrogation of the Hotel Detective, who his identification revealed was un Andre Morel. Morel's background check showed that indeed he was uniquely qualified in security work, but usually, it was because he had had run-ins with hotel security.

Morel had been arrested numerous times in the south of France for thefts in various high-profile hotels and casinos. Unfortunately, most of the time, the victims of his avarice, were convinced by Morel's lawyer that they would more likely regain their possessions if they dropped the charges. So, Morel had lots of activity on his record but no trials and no convictions.

What led Morel to Paris is what Boutin was trying to find out now. Perhaps they could get a lead on Marco.

Charles was concerned that the Renoir was at this very moment on its way out of the country. Marco had used Morel to distract the police while he got out of the D'Orsay with the original painting.

Charles realized that he hadn't reported to his superiors about his interrogation so far – frankly, he wasn't looking forward to another conversation with them today. They were pretty unhappy with the way things had turned out at the museum, but they also knew that he was their best and the only hope they had for recovering the missing artwork.

After speaking with Ellen and getting the information that Cathy and Eleanor had back safely, he decided to contact George Bertrand at the hotel and ask him to wait with the women while he brought his superiors up to date.

He asked Noelle, the commissioner's assistant to contact Bertrand for him to save time and went into the Commissioner's office. He had spent only a few minutes explaining what he'd learned from Morel when Noelle barged into the office and blurted out --

"Inspector Blanchard, I have tried to reach Officer Bertrand at the St. Jeanne, and the manager went to get him. He is not there!"

Not there? Why didn't Ellen tell him that on the call, Charles wondered? Bertrand's disappearance worried Charles, and he cut the commissioner's briefing short and quickly left the office.

"Noelle, contact Boutin in interrogation and tell him to meet me out front! And have my car brought around."

Charles met up with Boutin as he was getting into his city vehicle and sped off in the direction of the hotel. Crazy thoughts were racing through his mind as he sped through crowded streets around the Arc D'Triomphe. *Where was Bertrand? Was this a trap? Was Ellen under duress? How had Cathy and Eleanor managed to escape and get back to the hotel?* Boutin kept a hard eye on the road, warning Charles of pedestrians and other vehicles, occasionally gulping and appreciating the seat belt that kept him secure. He'd never seen Blanchard so anxious, and he knew that without a doubt his partner had fallen for the Americaine and was worried sick that something had happened to her.

"I should have come to the hotel straight away when I spoke with Ellen," Charles spoke out loud for the first time.

CHAPTER 27

I was still in the bathroom when Cathy opened the door. It was quiet, and I peered around the doorway to the sitting room. I noticed that Eleanor stood quietly by the French windows not noticing who Cathy admitted to the room. Expecting Charles Blanchard, I was shocked to see a man holding a gun on Cathy!

I didn't realize that Eleanor had turned around until I heard:

"How dare you, Albert! – Let her go, you young tuff! Put that gun down!"

I saw that Cathy was frightened but also knew something that Eleanor and the Albert did not – that I was in the bathroom, which meant that we had the element of surprise on him.

As I watched, he advanced on Eleanor - with the gun still at Cathy's side.

"Listen, old woman – you stay where you are, and your friend will be fine. You are cleverer than I gave you credit for but not clever enough. Do you think that you can get away that easily? I have friends in this hotel, and I was immediately contacted and told of your escape!"

Albert had been making his way with an irritated and frightened looking Cathy at his side until he stood in front of Eleanor and grinned. "D'Accord! It's back to the basement with you!"

Realizing that this situation could quickly erupt, I quietly made my way to the doorway to the sitting room and found tucked on the countertop in the dressing area the mostly empty bottle of wine from two nights ago - a messy but effective weapon, I supposed, as I crept forward. Eleanor, it seemed, was thinking too and suddenly she dropped in a faint to the ground.

Cathy cried out, "Eleanor!" and the

Albert, momentarily distracted allowed
Cathy to move away from him. He never
saw the blow that struck him down, his last
memory of being wet and seeing yellow.

CHAPTER 28

Charles pulled up in front of the hotel and was out of the car before the wheels had stopped turning. He was inside the hotel before the doorman could open the door and in the elevator before Boutin made it into the lobby. "Room 514!" he said as the elevator doors closed on Boutin's advancing form.

By the time Charles reached the fifth floor his gun was drawn and his breathing heavy.

He pushed the elevator doors aside quicker than they wanted to move and ran the 50 steps to the door of room 514.

As he reached the door he heard "Eleanor!" and that was enough for him. His elegantly shod foot connected with the unlocked door but by the time he got inside he found Cathy kneeling beside a spry looking Eleanor.

Ellen was standing over a young man dressed in a black leather jacket, holding a bottle of red wine, the floor around the perp littered with glass fragments and yellow tulips.

"What's happened here?" Charles demanded.

"A little bit of American justice is what I call it," exclaimed Eleanor who was now standing looking none the worse for wear.

"This young man is the one who kept us captive the last two days and shortly before you arrived, he came to the door, gun and all and made noises about locking us up in the basement again," Cathy explained while gingerly handing Charles, Albert's gun. "You'll probably want this....."

"Yes, so since he had a gun on Cathy, I figured we needed a distraction, so I pretended to faint and when Albert reacted

Cathy whacked him with the vase of tulips," Eleanor finished with a smirk.

"Yes, Charles, I saw it happen! I started to come out of the bathroom when I heard Eleanor's raised voice and grabbed this bottle of wine. But Cathy was too quick. As soon as Eleanor fainted and Albert reacted, Cathy reached for the flowers - like a wide receiver, by the way, and smashed it over his head in an instant! I am so proud of you Cathy!"

Charles wasn't looking at Ellen; instead, he was on the floor next to the unconscious man. He kept his knee in Albert's back as he went about handcuffing him.

"Ah, well-done mon frere'. I must be slowing down. You were up here and subduing a bad guy before I got to the elevator; a minimum of effort on my part." Boutin had entered the room as Charles was securing the handcuffs.

"A minimum of effort on my part as well, Boutin. The ladies meted out justice themselves!" His voice was light, but his posture betrayed Charles.

Now that the man was in custody, my adrenaline began to decrease, and I looked at Charles for the first time since he had busted into the room.

Charles stood rigid by the window as Boutin led Albert away. The hard look in his eye had erased the easygoing and charming Frenchman she met less than a week ago. In its place was a professional whose bearing exhibited tightly controlled anger.

I suppose that Charles is unaccustomed to victims taking matters into their own hands and I guess I understood.

But that wasn't it at all. Charles was alarmed at the escalation of events and the introduction of weapons into this ongoing crime spree. The kidnapping of Cathy and Eleanor had puzzled him, but he had told himself that Marco was merely ensuring that Charles went through with his end of the deal. But the man they had arrested the night before in the D'Orsay was armed, and now this one had been as well. *And why had Albert come back for the ladies? Why were they still intent on having Cathy and Eleanor hostage if the painting switch was complete?* There was something more to this case, convincing Charles that the ladies could no longer be considered safe. They must leave this city.

Observing him, I instinctively knew that he wasn't as blasé about what had transpired as he seemed. And neither was I.

As I began to reflect on all the events that had led to this point --- my accident, the burglary of our hotel room, the near hit-and-run involving Cathy, then the kidnapping of Cathy and Eleanor, I started to tremble in a small way, then my right eye began to twitch, and the room slowly swam before me.

"Ellen, are you alright? Charles had noticed that Ellen was unusually quiet, and he heard a gentle sloshing sound. When he looked at her, he could see that the sloshing was coming from the remnants of the bottle of wine in her hand, which was shaking. He rushed to her side and took the bottle out of her hand and placed his other hand gently on her arm, stopping its movement.

"Of course, I am, Charles. Not that you cared. You assigned an officer to me who ACTUALLY disappeared while guarding me. What could be wrong? I have never been better. The threat of kidnap and bodily harm is old news to me. Why did I ever think that this trip was going to be so good for me? People were so excited for me! Never been to Paris? Nope! See the sights, soak up the atmosphere! Why didn't they just say Good luck to you - come back in one piece!"

Ellen's voice became pitched and for the first-time Charles saw terror in them. As much as that upset him though, he saw it as an opportunity. Maybe with Ellen so scared he could convince her that the best thing to do would be to leave Paris.

"Ellen," Cathy too took note of Ellen's near hysteria and went to her side to comfort her. "Listen, it's over! The police have the detestable Albert in custody, and we are ok – all of us, and the thing now is to let the police take it from here."

She guided me to the bedroom and said over her shoulder "I think Ellen is tired and probably due for her pain medication. Let me get her settled, and I'll be back out."

Ten minutes later, Cathy reemerged from the bedroom and joined Eleanor and Charles in the sitting room. Eleanor had a glint in her eye, and Charles was trying to assure her that everything possible was being done to end this crime spree. And then, it occurred to her that she hadn't been in touch with her group of friends for two days.

"Dear Lord! Susan, Jessica, and the others must wonder what's become of us! We last saw them on the way to dinner two nights ago, and we never arrived. I've got to get a hold of them!"

"Dear Cathy, don't worry - I met your friends the other night after your abduction and can assure you that they are safe and they believe you are being kept out of sight until the case I am working on which threatened you, is resolved."

"The ladies left yesterday morning for England and will return to the United States as scheduled. They believe that you two and Ellen will join them in a day or so. I can only hope we can resolve things by then. In the meantime, I will find a safe place for the three of you. I would send you to join the others, but I am afraid that would only place all of you in jeopardy. But before you go anywhere, I need to debrief you about your kidnapping."

"We will be happy to fill you in on everything that happened. Anything we can do to move things along will benefit us, but Inspector, where does the investigation stand now? I know that Albert is not the kingpin of this little crime wave, so who is? Are you any closer to solving things?"

Cathy was trying to be helpful but had so many questions. Eleanor, quiet up until now, was trying to figure something out –

"Who is Marco? Is he the man you believe we're in danger from?"

"How do you know the name, Marco?" Charles asked with some trepidation.

"He is the older gentleman who brought us dinner last night in our basement hideaway. I am embarrassed to say he was quite attractive and for a moment…. Well never-mind." Cathy sputtered.

"He was the man who was behind our kidnapping. Only he seemed like a very decent type. Very respectful – if you can call a kidnapper respectful. However, he did lie to us. He told us he hadn't drugged our food, but something was doped. Perhaps the overly-sweet tea."

"Do you mean that you MET Marco?" Charles was astonished. What was Marco's game? In Charles' long experience with Marco and others like him, there was never any personal interaction.

At Charles' urging Cathy and Eleanor recounted the time Marco spent with them and also the details from the kidnapping. Charles listened to every word but was thinking all the time. This whole scenario was out of character with Marco. In his past dealings with the thief, Marco had always been 'in and out fast.' He involved no one else and barely left evidence behind. This time it was like he was going out of his way to leave evidence, dangling clues, almost like he was playing with the authorities.

Besides, the increasingly violent nature of this spree was not what Marco normally would be involved in. Of course, it had been ten years since a crime had occurred with Marco's 'signature.' *Why would he come back now*? He could have taken the Renoir without involving Charles or the French authorities at all. And what had happened to young Officer Bertrand? He had been put in place to guard Ellen's door because he was so trustworthy; where had he gone?

Charles needed a lot of answers, and he feared he was running out of time. Marco may well have fled by now.

The first thing to do was to get the women to safety.

CHAPTER 29

I was still very drowsy when Cathy quietly shook me awake and told me we were leaving.

"But it's not Friday – we're not leaving until Friday," I muttered.

"Honey, we have to leave. Charles says that we are not safe here and is taking us somewhere where we will be. I have packed up your things, and Eleanor is with a policewoman packing hers right now. I need you to pull it together and get up. We need to leave within the next 15 minutes." Cathy explained without letting on how concerned she was. She was also exhausted, having spent a harrowing few days, but the urgency with which Charles was treating their departure had activated her adrenaline, and she felt she could move mountains at that moment to protect her niece and her friend, Eleanor.

"Where are Jessica, Susan, and the others?" I wanted to know and struggled to get up from the bed.

"They have continued to London. Charles thought it would be best and they left yesterday." Cathy explained.

"Now, please we must go!"

"Where is Charles taking us?" I wondered. I was so tired, bone weary and dizzy from the medication and the sudden wake-up. As I sat on the edge of the bed, trying to still my buzzing head, Charles walked into the room and said,

"Ma petite, I am taking you to a place where security is not an issue. A place that has barriers which will keep the people who are after you – out!"

"You're taking us to jail?" Ellen exclaimed. Charles could not hold back a whoop of laughter – "No dear, I would fear for the guards. I am taking you to an historic, but very safe and beautiful place and I will say no more…"

CHAPTER 30

I managed to get cleaned up and within ten minutes or so we were leaving the hotel through the backdoor, in a limousine with tinted windows. Charles had considered a service van of some kind to spirit them away but considering the hard time the three women had endured over the past several days, decided they deserved a bit of luxury. So, Charles had contacted his driver and instructed him to bring the car to the back of the hotel. The ladies would enjoy the long ride in comfort.

Despite my curiosity at where Charles was taking us for our safety, I was exhausted and spent the long limo ride in a drug-induced, sleep-deprived, healing sleep. So, when I finally awoke, I found myself on a very comfy bed in an elegant little room. I gingerly sat up and assessed how I felt – arm: ok; head: a bit fuzzy; but all of me was beginning to feel strong,

Then I noticed I wasn't alone in the room. Cathy was stretched out on the chaise across the room. The windows were dark. Night must have fallen in the time I'd slept.

Cathy heard Ellen stirring and woke herself.

 "Well, sleeping beauty, finally you wake up!" Cathy said with some relief.

A quick look at my watch confirmed that I'd had slept for more than 14 hours. It was now just after 4 in the morning, and the others in the house were sound asleep, despite the excitement at their location.

"Where are we?" I asked without the whine that had framed my previous similar question.

"Mont Saint-Michel," Cathy said with a hint of excitement.

"Mont Saint-Michel? What are we doing here?" I was groggy and thought I might have been day-dreaming... "This wasn't on the tour."

Cathy must have realized I was still a bit disoriented. "Yes, I know, but Charles has brought us here to his 'retreat' she explained.

"This is his home?" I was surprised.

Cathy hastened to explain, "Well, not so much his home as, his home-away-from-home -- it was left to him by an old, dear, friend and he felt we would be safe here because it is an historic fortress. Once the tide comes in, it will be difficult to access."

"But didn't I read that that only happens twice a month?" I asked.

"Well, in addition, he has posted guards at the causeway entrance, and there are guards at our door." Cathy wasn't too happy about that, but she understood the need. I could tell that Cathy was disturbed by the extra 'escorts' but hearing that I began to relax for the first time in two days.

"You, know Cathy you never did tell me what happened to you and Eleanor."

By the time Cathy had finished the story, and I had related my own, dawn was beginning to break. We stood in silence and watched the sun rise over the Bay of Mont-Saint-Michel.

"Do you think we can go outside and watch the sunrise?" I asked. Cathy, probably knowing that Charles would say no, suggested that I ask the guard at the door. There would be no harm done if he said no and she thought that it would be a wonderful memory to have.

At her assent, I went to the door and quietly opened it, mindful that there were others asleep in the house. "Pardon…" I began surprised when the guard lifted his drooping head, and it was, in fact, Charles.

"Charles, what are you doing guarding the door? Don't you have officers who can do this for you? You must not have slept in days. How are you going to catch the bad guys if you're wiped out?"

"Oh, so many questions…Well, may I first say Bonjour! It looks like you've had a good rest. I have as well. It's my shift on guard duty, but I assure you that I got a good eight hours during your nap," Charles answered.

I heard a lift in his voice -- clearly, he was rested. As for myself, I felt like I was in control again. That fragility I had felt yesterday after the capture of Albert was gone, and I felt good.

"Good, I'm glad you finally got some rest, and I am glad to see you. Cathy and I were wondering if there were a chance, we could watch the sunrise over the bay from outside."

"Well, I think I could arrange that – and you're probably famished, aren't you?"

With that Charles spoke into the cell phone he held in his hand – after a babble of French which I didn't understand, he slapped it closed and said – "go get your Aunt, and we shall go out onto the terrace and have breakfast and watch the sun come up!"

"Thank you!" I didn't waste a moment, but when I got into the room, Cathy was curled up on the bed snoring softly.

Leaving her a note as to my whereabouts – I wasn't taking any more chances, I left the room and found Charles waiting outside, in quiet conversation with another man.

"Ellen, this is Georges Bertrand, you will probably remember him as the guard who disappeared from your door at the St. Jeanne…" Charles explained.

"Yes, I remember you very well – where did you disappear to?" I asked.

"I'll explain that to you at breakfast. Charles interjected. "Where is your aunt?"

"She's sleeping – I couldn't bear to wake her."

"D'accord, Georges will take my place here until I come back." Charles determined.

"No offense, Officer Bertrand, but Charles – he disappeared before – what makes you think he won't again? Is Cathy safe here – with him?"

"Very safe, ma petite. I have had Georges' explanation for his disap-pearance, and I trust it implicitly. Come, let's go to breakfast."

Charles gave a light tug on my good arm and led me down the quiet hallway. We passed a darkened living room and dining room. As we approached a wall, Charles withdrew a remote from his pocket and pressed a button. The wall was covered floor to ceiling with heavy drapes and as they opened Ellen noticed that the wall was entirely made of French doors and overlooked the bay.

Charles unlocked the door to the terrace, and we stepped outside. I had expected that it would be a bit cool, considering that it was only April, but it was surprisingly warm. There was a faint pink glow over the bay as the sun rose in the sky and the rhythmic pull of the tide made me relax instantly.

Charles escorted me to a table at the right of the terrace, and I sat down. "How beautiful this is – I wish I could take a photograph and keep it with me forever. I shall ne-ver forget it," I said betraying my emotion with a catch in my voice…

The bay seemed to stretch into infinity, and the sunrise was an impressionistic masterpiece of palest lilac to pink then orange and a soft lemony yellow as if promising a beautiful day.

I could feel Charles watching me, and I knew that he felt way I did as well. The moderate tension in the set of my shoulders and chin was washing away – relaxing for the first time in days. Charles had relaxed too -- finally!

"Alors, mon Coeur -- let me check on breakfast. Don't move a muscle. I'll be right back."

Charles had to escape the intimacy of the terrace for a moment. It was exciting and a relief to him to see how relaxed Ellen was becoming. Watching the sunrise with her was, without doubt, a moment he'd never forget. And when she closed her eyes, a tiny tear emerged from her bottom lid, and Charles knew he was in love with her. The Ellen he had met less than a week ago had gone from clutzy, funny and sometimes highly strung to a woman who was not afraid to be her true self. She was a romantic.

Charles' ruminations were interrupted by his assistant and chef, Alain, approaching with the tray of food and coffee.

Bon! I was just coming to see where breakfast was. I'll get the door for you." With that, Charles returned through the living room and pulled open the French door.

I smiled up as Charles followed by a tall, well-built younger man carrying a tray emerged onto the terrace.

"Ellen, this is my assistant Alain. He has prepared a light breakfast for us." Charles explained as he moved aside to allow Alain room to place the tray on the low table in front of me.

"Merci Alain. That will be all." Charles resumed his seat beside me, and Alain drew away without a word, leaving Charles and me alone.

"Lovely," I said as I took in the breakfast tray. It was laden with a vase of fresh lilacs and lovely white china; a basket covered with a pale lilac cloth covering what I assumed to be fresh croissants – for I could smell them; a pitcher of orange juice and a porcelain coffeepot; emitting the unmistakable aroma of fresh coffee and small dishes of glistening jams.

Charles was grateful for the care Alain had taken to ensure that this moment with Ellen was perfect.

Charles watched me, and I watched Charles, each knowing that this was a turning point in our friendship and also that the mood could so soon be broken. Neither one of us wanted to speak, so we didn't. Spontaneously, I moved my chair closer to him and reached for his hand, squeezed it gently and finally said, "thank you."

Charles was touched.

"You are very welcome, ma petite. I am glad you are here." With that, the spell should have broken, but we continued to hold hands and watch the sunrise.

Several minutes later, Charles said, "Well, how about a cup of cafe?"

"Yes, please! Suddenly I'm starving!" I realized I hadn't eaten since the late morning of the day before and finally with a clear head I was hungry!

We continued to sit side by side and enjoy our breakfast together. I made up for the lack of calories over the past day by polishing off three croissants!

Charles ate well, for he found himself relaxing too. The past days of worry and heightened tension had taken a toll on him.

We spoke quietly, and Charles told me how he had come to own the house on the Mont.

"My grandfather died young – at fifty-five -- and my grandmother who was from Normandy crawled into a shell. They had had a wonderful marriage, and she was desolate to lose him so young. Nothing could be done, and she withdrew from us. At a certain point, we became concerned for her because it had been several years since he died, and she seemed to have died with him. So, her sister who was a nun came to her and told her that she needed a change. The two of them came to this island and stayed in this house, which belonged to a family my great-aunt knew.

Day by day my grandmother began to emerge from her shell – first noticing the beauty of the abbey and the ancient buildings, and ever so slowly she began to lighten up.

One day she was walking the beach and talking to heaven, to my grandfather. She told me she asked him if he were still with her and if he was at peace. She said the answer came to her in a rush of the waves – having lost track of time she realized the tide was coming in and as Grand-mere started to run she got her foot stuck in the wet sand.

The tide, which is rumored to come in 'as swiftly as a galloping horse' pummeled her, and she felt sure she was going to drown when all of a sudden, she was lifted free from the sand.

Her rescuer was Bernard, the son of this house, and he and she married after several months. Grand-mere told me that she felt my grandfather 'gave her' Bernard. They were happy together and died here within days of each other after more than thirty years of marriage. I grew up here. We divided the year between our house in the city and holidays and summers here on the Mont. I love it here. I was left the house in Bernard's will."

Ellen was touched by the story and grateful for Charles sharing it with her.

"It's amazing. There is something about this place which heals you." I said softly. "I feel it."

"I feel it too," Charles whispered. And with that, he leaned over and kissed me as I'd wanted him to do for days. It wasn't a shy or uncertain kiss or a brief one at that.

After several moments we drew apart and Charles – awkward now, said, "I have never experienced anything like this with anyone! I believe I know now what my grandmother was fortunate enough to have found twice."

"Charles, what are you saying?" I whispered, thunderstruck that perhaps he felt what I was feeling. But at that moment Cathy arrived on the terrace and the moment was over.

There was a momentary awkwardness when Cathy came out -- I could tell she felt like she had interrupted something. Her eyes darted back and forth between the two of us. To ease the moment Charles welcomed her and seated Cathy in the chair to my left and then rang a small crystal bell for Alain to bring more coffee and croissants.

Charles and I were somewhat grateful for the interruption because those moments before had surprised us so. We needed to absorb what had occurred and think about what was next.

Eleanor soon joined our threesome, and we had a lively breakfast. Everyone was feeling so much lighter that Charles was hesitant to remind them that they were there because it was a place of safety and that he must get to work solving the case.

"Well my lovely friends, we must, I'm afraid, discuss what comes next. I brought you here because it is safe, and you have been in too much danger. Unfortunately, the threat to you remains until I can resolve things. So, I have to return to Paris and pick up the thread where it was left. If I waste too much time, Marco and the Renoir will disappear forever."

"I trust you, Charles, you know that, but with you gone, will we be safe here? I know that this is a fortress, but anyone can get in over the causeway. What is to prevent Marco and his henchmen from coming here?"

The tension was beginning to build again in me, and Charles hated to see it.

"Officer Bertrand is accompanied by several others including two men manning the causeway. Alain too is here to protect you. He is former military and will see you are safe. As for Officer Bertrand, I guarantee you that you can trust him. The reason that he left the hotel is that he got a phone call – purportedly from me telling him I had captured Marco and the coast was clear. That was not me, but someone impersonating me. I have arranged a code with my men including Bertrand, and such a mistake will not happen again. Please feel secure." Charles explained gently.

"We do." I said with some relief. But I was concerned for Charles and said so.

"What about you? Aren't you in danger from Marco?" I asked.

"Well, I consider that to be a job requirement. These men are not so much dangerous but determined. We have young Albert in custody, and at this moment my enthusiastic colleague, Boutin is questioning him. Albert will break, I assure you."

I was becoming tense, but I wasn't sure if it was because Charles would be in danger or because after growing so close, I feared it was an aberration and things would return to normal between us.

"Charles, how about keeping Eleanor and Cathy here to recuperate, and I will go with you. I'm feeling so much stronger, and I know I'll be helpful to you." I asked.

"No mon amie, you stay here and try to have a vacation. That's why you came to France. Alain or Bertrand can see you around the Mont - although of course, it would probably be a good idea to go when it is busiest - so you can blend into the crowd. You will be safe here, and that will help me to work better. I will know that I don't have to worry about you although I do believe that I will have to warn Alain and Bertrand about your ability to get into trouble," Charles said with a hint of laughter.

It was difficult for him to leave also. Ellen was becoming very important to him, and he wanted her to be safe.

"Hilarious, Charlie.   I'm a changed woman. I just thought since I'd been in on this from the beginning, I could help you catch the bad guy. But I know that you're the real-life incarnation of Inspector Clouseau, so I will let you get on with it."

I was sassing him shamelessly and could see he was enjoying it. But Charles knew that to enjoy her for many years to come (and that's what he was beginning to realize, he wanted) he needed to go.

Fifteen minutes later I walked Charles to the front door. Cathy and Eleanor, realizing we'd want a few minutes alone together, remained in the living room.

At the door, I reached out and grabbed Charles's arm and turned him to face me.

"From the moment I met you I have not only been fascinated by you, but I've also enjoyed your company very much.   I appreciate all that you have done in protecting me and my friends but know this. I feel responsible for you having the problems on this case you've had, and I am sorry for that.   I'm not talking just about the complications I have caused but also that things seem to have gotten worse for you with me around.

The only reason I am staying here – and I will behave, is so that you can solve this case and come back safely. I know art thefts are not supposed to be dangerous, so something else has to be going on. Be safe. When you return safely, I will sleep well. Until you do, I will toss and turn and wonder what you are doing. So, please don't delay. You know I need my rest."

That last said with a slight laugh. I was putting it all on the table. I had to stop myself from telling Charles that I loved him, but I did. I'd gone from mere interest in Ma Whistler's great-grandson to having daydreams of our lives together. But I didn't want to be the first to say I love you. If Charles did, he would tell me. I just knew it.

Charles was taken aback by Ellen's farewell words and momentarily contemplated leaving the solving of the case to Boutin and his superiors so that he could stay here with Ellen. He knew though that with so much on the line – his career, the priceless painting and his future with Ellen, he had to go himself.

"My darling girl, we have been through much together, but don't fool yourself that there is that much danger. I will wrap it up quickly. As I told you, usually these things are more about strategy and less about violence. It seems Marco has been trying to get my attention over the last week. He has done that, and I will see that this case is resolved. I hate to leave you – especially since you now are willing to behave – I'd like to see that myself. But I will be back soon. Au Revoir, mon Coeur.

After Charles left, I ran back to my room and dug out my French-English dictionary and looked up mon Coeur.

CHAPTER 31

Charles used his personal car to return to Paris. He wanted the limousine to stay at the Mont on the chance that Ellen, Cathy, and Eleanor needed it. What they didn't realize is that the limo was bullet-proof. The women knew very little about him. They would be surprised about his upbringing.

While he had told Ellen a bit this morning, he did not feel it would be wise to let her know from what a distinguished family he came. When he did choose to tell her, he was afraid of her reaction.

His family was well entrenched in French Society and she would either find that appealing or appalling. He knew she had a very typical middle-class background. How would she react to his wealth? While he wasn't ashamed of it, he didn't want it to be the reason she stayed in France.

Charles also worried about her reaction to Marco's true identity. He didn't know how he would be able to keep it from her. Once he was captured, the news would be all over the papers. She wouldn't be able to avoid it. Unless he managed to solve the case and deal with Marco privately.

His final concern was the second thoughts he was having about bringing these women to the Mont - a place Charles knew Marco was intimately familiar with. He satisfied himself with the notion that Marco was surely concentrating now on getting out of France. Marco had the Hassam painting and presumably the Renoir. He wouldn't be going to a place so connected to him that Charles would be looking for him there.

These thoughts weighed heavily on him as he drove back to Paris, driving directly to headquarters to look in on how the questioning of Albert was going.

On his arrival, Boutin greeted him with the news that Albert was singing like a choir boy.

"What did he say the plan was, Boutin? Did he say where Marco is hiding out? Does he know what he intends to do with the Renoir?" Charles demanded.

"No, my friend, he is just a flunky, but he did tell me when the next meet is scheduled, and I am happy you are back. He is to meet with Marco tonight at Les Halles in the Church of St Eustace." Boutin explained with satisfaction. He had done his job, but it had been a very long night.

"What time are they to meet?" Charles asked with relief.

And Boutin told him "10 pm."

"I'd like to speak with Albert myself," Charles stated.

"Ah, don't trust me, mon amie?" Boutin asked.

"I trust you with my life, but I wonder if perhaps some different questions will throw Albert off and force him to reveal more. I intend to try." Charles said with determination.

Charles was worried about the planned meeting at Les Halles. He needed another plan on the chance that Marco failed to show.

Boutin took advantage of Charles' arrival to go home and get some rest. After he left, Charles looked over the transcript of Albert's interrogation and that of Andre Morel, the former hotel detective at the St. Jeanne. He hoped to find similarities or inconsistencies to exploit as he interviewed Albert again, spending more than an hour reading the transcripts over twice. On his third try, Charles found it. Morel had mentioned that he met Marco at a funeral for a 'friend' in Nice. And Albert was originally from Nice but claimed that he left there after the death of a family member.

So, Nice was a connection, but was it possible that the funeral Marco and Morel attended tied to Albert? And what would be significant to know is whose funeral it was. To attract three thieves, there had to be some crime involved; perhaps the dead man was a colleague.

Charles asked Noelle, the commissioner's assistant to do some research while he took his daily trip to the d'Orsay. When he returned, there would be answers.

CHAPTER 32

I didn't like being left behind regardless of the beauty of Mont St. Michel. My aunt and Eleanor seemed happy enough to stay put and putter around the Mont, but there were restrictions. The ladies, according to Officer Bertrand could only go at the height of the day when the majority of the tourists were out. An irony, of course, since one would expect that having a house on the Mont you could take advantage of the lighter tourist times. But those were the restrictions that Charles had imposed. They all understood it, of course, but I chose to stay put and let

Eleanor and Cathy tour without me. I was holding out for a personal sundown tour with a certain inspector when he returned.

Alain stayed at the house with me, and with time on my hands, I decided to look around and see where Charles 'got away from it all.'

Lovely house, not overly masculine, I thought to myself. I peeked in what I assumed was the master bedroom, the primary color, being the palest of blues. Creamy accents in the pillows and bedclothes played off the deep azure of the drapes. On the large wall facing the king-sized bed was a stunning print of Van Gogh's Olive Trees. The print was handsomely framed and gave the impression of being an original. Nice touch with the frame, I thought.

I wandered then around the other rooms on the second floor and then returned to the first floor. The thing that impressed me the most about the home was its' accessibility. It looked like a home that is lived in and loved. There were comfortable throws over the chairs in the bedroom and living rooms. The tables were laden with personal treasures alongside current books and magazines.

The last room on the first floor was Charles's office. The walls were a highly glossed brown and the drapes at the floor to ceiling windows, a cream brocade. Here beautiful black and white photographs hung on the walls and were lovingly placed on occasional tables. The desk was a simple black tabletop with long tapered legs. And sitting in the middle of it was a laptop computer.

It had occurred to me that some research might help Charles in his search for Marco. Perhaps that could be her contribution. The laptop was just the tool she needed!

With Alain in the kitchen preparing dinner, I figured I had about 45 minutes to do some research. If he came in, I'd tell him I was bored and surfing the web.

When the computer booted up, I decided to see if the Google or Yahoo search engines would work in France and, sure enough, despite the language barrier, they did!

I searched recent art thefts + Marco. There were references to a large, costly art heist in Zurich, but the robbery she wanted information about happened ten years ago. Further research did bring up an article about a heist in a famous French museum but did not mention a Hassam or Marco. I wasn't getting anywhere until I decided to search for Blanchard + Art Heist + Hassam.

There it was, a reference to several articles over a period of 6 months. The first article reported the crime and indicated that Insp.

Charles Blanchard was in charge of the investigation.

There was a follow-up to an article regarding a leak on the case, the leaker purporting that someone very close to the investigation had a personal knowledge and relationship with the thief. I was beginning to get a very sick feeling in my stomach. I knew now what the remaining articles would reveal – that Charles was related to the thief, Marco!

CHAPTER 33

On Charles' return from the d'Orsay, Noelle did have some news for him. Morel and Marco had met at the funeral of Gerard LaVergne. LaVergne was a legendary thief, with a rap sheet going back more than 50 years. Although he had never dabbled seriously in high-end art theft, he had been implicated in numerous thefts of jewelry in the south of France. He was known as the Cat Ferrat, because of his nighttime raids on tony homes in Cap Ferrat. As a cat burglar, he was unmatched, yet he maintained an outward identity as a famous restauranteur in Nice.

During the late 1960s, the Cat was not heard from, and that coincided with the period that LaVergne served in prison.

Noelle also found out that while serving time he shared a cell with Albert's stepfather – Luc Morel. This was useful information. All that they had known to date about Albert was his family name – Jetter.

Albert's father. Denis Jetter had been a thug and a thief who ultimately turned on the gang of criminals he associated with and was killed for his troubles. His wife Sophie married Luc Morel very shortly after his death and by all accounts was not particularly disturbed by her brief widowhood. She and Luc did have a love match and though it produced no children, Albert, only eight at the time of his father's death idolized Luc Morel and eventually took his stepfather's name. When he was nineteen, however, he began to run with the wrong crowd. Morel who had been 15 years out of prison and pursuing legitimate business, told Albert that he could no longer use the Morel name if he were considering a life of crime. Rather than having the effect of curing Albert of pursuing that seamy life, it worked to free him to raise hell under an alias – his birth name, Albert Jetter.

Morel had, during his first marriage to a fishwife named Claudine, produced another burden to society – Andre Morel, who was currently cooling his heels about 100 feet away. The recently 'retired' hotel detective Morel and Albert were two cells apart and had no idea the other was in custody. Perhaps Charles could work with that.

What Noelle had limited information on and was continuing to pursue, was the connection of Marco, Albert, and Morel to Gerard LaVergne, now deceased master thief. Until he had hard facts from Noelle, Charles would have to pursue his hunch – that LaVergne had employed Albert and Morel to surveil his targets and or help him move the stolen jewelry. When LaVergne died, Marco was on the scene and became their new employer. Marco would have known LaVergne despite the difference in their targets. They were known to operate in the same region, and both counted on the very wealthy residents of that broad area to provide their income.

"Now, which one of those two pathetic losers would be the easiest to exploit?" Charles said out loud. "Albert," he concluded and then phoned the jailer to move him to an interrogation room.

Albert had had a tough night. He had been knocked out by a 70-year-old woman, hauled into jail and interrogated all night by nasty Boutin, who continued to mock him as weak and a loser. Charles knew that was how Boutin conducted the interview because he had read the transcripts of the interrogation and also because he knew that was how his friend and partner operated. He wanted to remove any form of pride and ego from his subject which would allow him to convince the weakened man to spill his guts.

When Charles entered the interrogation room, Albert was seated with his hands cuffed behind him and his forehead touching the table. Charles kicked the table leg and said "Allo …. Allo! – are you sleepy my friend? I would think that you have plenty of time to sleep – don't do it on my time! You owe me some information, Albert, and we are not leaving here until I get it. You see the information you provided to my Amie Boutin was information we had already – the 10 pm appointment is old news. So, if you wish to have any sleep in the next week or two, I suggest you come up with something else!" Charles knew that he was taking the risk that Albert would make something up to avoid providing real information, but he would start here and hope that he could bluff enough to get Albert to tell him whatever he wanted.

Albert had lifted his head when Charles kicked the table and looked at him through bleary eyes. "Cochon – what do you want? I told your friend that bastard Boutin all that I knew, and he seemed satisfied. That's all you get too!"

"Well Albert, Boutin was also tired, and he did not have the information about you that I have now. And, from reading the transcripts, it seems he neglected to remind you about the prison time you're facing. Kidnapping is very serious, and two counts are surely enough to keep you in prison until you face that final, permanent nap. And, with what your friend Morel told me about your involvement in the attacks on the Americaine and her friends and your role in plotting the theft from the D'Orsay the other night, I am convinced that you have breathed your last free breath!"

"Morel – what do you know of him?" Albert asked suspiciously.

"Well, from what Morel told me he was following your orders when he entered the d'Orsay on Tuesday night, and you are the one who knows where the painting is," Charles drawled.

"Well, that pig lied to you – how do you even know Morel?" Albert spat.

"Albert, this is not your lucky day. Morel is in custody and laid out the whole plan for us." Charles said.

CHAPTER 34

I was anxious. The remaining articles I'd found in my internet search had not confirmed my original suspicions. Blanchard had categorically denied his relationship with the thief, Marco to the reporter and an inquiry had confirmed that he was telling the truth. But I could usually trust my gut, and it was telling me that this series of crimes seemed to be designed to taunt Charles.

If Charles was pursuing the thief and the thief was indeed Marco, there was every chance that Charles' life was in danger. The articles I'd found on the internet seemed to indicate that Marco was from an aristocratic family but that his parents had shunned him after he developed a penchant for acquiring art under suspicious circums-tances. This family was well entrenched in French Society and could trace their bloodline back to various royals.

Playing a hunch, I did a new Google search; one for Marco Blanchard.

The results were surprising. Hundreds of results came up for hundreds of Blanchards – even one for a deceased Charles Blanchard, but none for Marco Blanchard.

Out of curiosity and with a sick feeling, I followed a link to a story about the late Charles Blanchard. That one turned out to be Charles' father and confirmed that he had died at the age of 55 leaving a wife, a son and a sister. The sister's married name was Duclos and it mentioned she had a son, Marc. I wondered if that Marc Duclos could now be rogue and art thief – Marco.

Following that trail filled me with dread – *what would I do if the cause of all our troubles here in France was related to the man I wanted to marry?*

A footfall in the hallway ended my analysis and by the time Alain came into view I was curled up on the chaise, deeply engrossed in a book on Mont St. Michel.

CHAPTER 35

Albert was a very weak man, Charles had concluded. After Charles' intense interrogation of Albert, he spilled his guts. The topper, the thing that convinced him more than any other tactic that Charles had used, was Luc Morel. After mentioning that Andre Morel was also in custody, Charles had played a hunch.

"Yes, your dear stepbrother is also our guest, and he has company coming – you remember Luc Morel don't you, Albert?"

Charles had figured that even after all these years Albert still valued the opinion of the man who had helped raise him, then disowned him. Because his stepfather disavowed him and told Albert he could no longer consider himself a Morel, he needed a new name. Why not take another name as an alias – instead he, perhaps through a lack of imagination or perhaps as an act of self-loathing, had taken the name of the trash who fathered him – Jetter.

After offering him the chance to meet with Luc Morel – the only decent man he'd had in his life – Albert, worn down by his failures and certain his nasty stepbrother would turn him in first, blew the whistle on the whole plan.

Tonite at 10 pm, Marco, would be waiting inside St. Eustache, and Charles would be there to capture him.

CHAPTER 36

Alain didn't seem surprised to find me on the chaise in Charles' office reading a book about Mont St. Michel, which was a relief, but he withdrew quickly after ascertaining that I didn't want anything to eat or drink.

'I don't know why I feel so guilty -- there are many other things I could do with a laptop, besides poking my nose into Charles' investigation. For all Alain knew I could be researching the history of the Mont or checking shop listings to see if there was a place, I could get a manicure. But I knew the guilt was entirely of my creation, for I believed that I'd discovered something about Charles that he wouldn't want me to know.'

That fact made me angry, for he should have told me – *told me when? When he was hauling me out of the fountain, or putting me in the safe hands of Georges and Jacqueline while he hunted for Eleanor and Cathy? Certainly, the time had not been right.* I was worried that perhaps his reticence with that information had more to do with his concern for protecting his 'cousin' Marco than with fully disclosing the information to the woman he loved – me.

Another worry I had was that Charles was in danger and that despite his protestations to the contrary – that Marco would resort to violence to protect his freedom. And, perhaps I was wrong about the relationship between Charles and Marco. If Marco had no familial ties to Charles, would he be more likely to react violently? All of these questions pointed out my major flaw – not my slightly wide hips or my clumsiness, nor indeed my penchant for getting into trouble – but the over-analysis of every situation – the worrying of every detail.

I could work myself into a state of panic in the time a normal girl could polish off a chocolate bar! Even knowing that about myself, I couldn't pull back the worry. I knew that if I had any chance of a future with Charles, I had to find a way to help him – and I couldn't do it from here.

I needed a plan tout-suite!

I thought much better when I was moving so I went to the kitchen to find Alain and tell him I wanted a tour of the Mont.

Approaching the kitchen, I could hear Alain's cell phone ring, and I paused while he answered it. I hoped it was Charles and that I could get some information from their conversation. The problem would be translating those details from French to English in the time it took Alain to repeat them.

"Allo? Oui, Msr. – Oui, she is 'ere in the study reading. But what shall I do about the ladies… oui, I understand you need my help – oui, I am sure that Bertrand can 'andle the ladies. D'accord, I will meet you there." With that Alain hung up the phone and went in search of Bertrand's cell number.

Out of sight in the hallway, I realized that this was a perfect solution. I could hide in the car and 'accompany' Alain to his meeting with Charles.

Charles would be upset that I came along, but once he realized that I could be helpful, he would forgive me.

It was important to me that I see this through. I'd been in the middle of this little crime wave and couldn't stand the thought that I wouldn't be present for its conclusion.

CHAPTER 37

Charles was not going to wait until 10 pm to meet Marco. He knew that the Church of St. Eustace was a busy location, but there were many places he could seclude himself. If Marco were aware of the capture of Albert and Morel, he would fear the meeting was a trap. Charles needed to be in place before the meeting.

From what Albert had told him, Marco was getting ready to flee with his ill-gotten Renoir and was meeting Albert to arrange his departure from France. What Charles was concerned about was the location of his buyer and if that buyer had the Hassam, stolen by Marco years before.

Charles had been very successful in his career with the Suretè, but that one unsolved case had haunted him for years. It was a blemish on his professional record, but it was also a matter of family pride. His family had loaned the Hassam to the Louvre several generations before and so retrieving it and seeing it hanging in its rightful spot was a matter of honor to him.

Albert had mentioned that Marco was likely to turn up for the meeting early so that he could surveil the area for the authorities. He suggested that his employer was treating this job with a seriousness he hadn't displayed in previous heists.

"Alors, cochon! You'll 'ave your 'ands full with him. You'd think this was his own treasure he was taking!" Albert warned.

"Yes, quite so." Charles drawled. He knew how personal it was to both of them.

CHAPTER 38

I waited for Alain to return to the study and tell me he was leaving. I planned to tell him that I'd already arranged to go at noon and meet the ladies for lunch on the Mont. Then when he was about to get in the car, I'd run out ready to "meet Bertrand," tell him there was a phone call and while he went in to answer it, hide in the back of the car.

Alain will not expect to see me, because he'll think I had gone to meet Bertrand. I mused, pleased with my plan.

"Mademoiselle,"

I was so intent on my plan I didn't realize Alain had come into the room.

"Mademoiselle, I have been ordered back to Paris and have arranged for Bertrand to come back to the house and collect you. He thought he would take you and the ladies to lunch at one of the café's here in the Mont. He should be back here in 15 or 20 minutes – at Noon, and then I shall leave."

I couldn't believe my luck.

Why, it's like I'm psychic. Alain was following my plan to the letter, and I hadn't shared it with him.

"Why, that's fine Alain. I can meet Bertrand if he wishes at the bottom of the lane."

"Non, m'selle, I insist on waiting with you. Msr. Blanchard has ordered me to do so and a few minutes more or less will make no difference to my arrangements."

God! I thought to myself. Lighten up Alain!

Obviously, Alain's military training had equipped him for a life of following orders to the nth degree. And I knew he wouldn't waver from his orders. What was I going to do to distract him with Bertrand there as well as Eleanor and Cathy?

I had to think of something!

"Well, I'll go upstairs and freshen up for lunch." If the others get back here before I do, please tell them I'll be right down." I left the room and ascended the staircase to my room.

Once there, I paced back and forth and finally came up with a plan I thought could work.

I picked up the house phone and called the kitchen.

"Alain, I think I will skip lunch. All of a sudden, I am so tired and achy. Can you ask Bertrand to return here with my Aunt and Eleanor? Perhaps they can have lunch while I nap?"

"Oui, mademoiselle. Of course. Do you need me to send for a doctor?" Alain asked with a tone I found obnoxious ... like he thought I was lying.

"No, thank you for your concern, but I am drained. Please give the others my apologies for being a wet blanket, but it's been a very trying week for me. I think it's just caught up with me."

"Oui, I will contact Bertrand immediately."

I waited about 5 minutes before leaving the room. I tiptoed down the stairs, listening for Alain's footsteps. The front door was closed, and I wondered if it would make noise if I opened it. I decided to risk it.

I quietly approached the door, and at that moment the phone rang, stopping me in my tracks and causing a knife-like pain in my stomach. Then I realized that this was my opportunity.

Alain answered the house phone on the second ring, and while he was tied up, I slid out the front door to the limo.

CHAPTER 39

On the floor in the back seat of the limo, I found a black throw. I managed to hide under it and waited for Alain, forcing myself to take long, relaxing breaths. I knew that the moment Alain got into the car to leave, I'd have to breathe as shallowly as possible and be as quiet as possible.

I wish I were awake for more of that drive down here yesterday, I thought. *I don't know how long it took – an hour or 3 hours, and I wish I'd thought to go to the bathroom before sneaking in here.*

I took a moment to assess the condition of my bladder and decided I was ok for now. Fortunately for me, the floor of the limo was flat, and I'd laid down on my right side so that my sore shoulder was on top and not being crushed beneath me.

The throw I'd chosen was lovely black wool. The label was in my eyeline – *cashmere – of course*, I chuckled. But it was long and full enough to cover me entirely and blend into the interior of the car.

At that moment I heard a car drive up and Alain, who must have been waiting at the door, said "Miss Devlin is napping, she has asked that you lunch without her. There is a Salade Nicoise on the counter, and the vinaigrette is in the fridge and will need a quick whisk. Rolls are in a low oven, and there is tea prepared and ready to pour. Msr. is expecting me to meet him in Paris in two hours. I don't expect we'll be back this evening. Ladies, please enjoy your lunch. I am sure you can arrange something for dinner."

Officer Bertrand acknowledged Alain's instructions. "Oui, tell Blanchard we'll be fine. I will see the ladies have a proper meal tonight and tomorrow morning. Good luck, Alain."

"Oh, yes, this will be a lovely break. Are you sure Ellen is all right?" Ellen heard Cathy ask.

"Oui madame, she claims to be tired. I'm sure she'll be eager to eat when she awakes," Alain commented a bit sarcastically. With that Alain got into the car and started it up. He took off with a scatter of gravel, jostling me out of my comfortable position onto my left arm. I smothered a scream by biting onto the black cashmere throw.

After what I estimated to be about 50 minutes, Alain's cell phone rang, and I slowed my breathing so that I could hear the conversation.

Unfortunately, my French was not up to the rapid-fire exchange.

So, the conversation was beyond me. I listened for any mention of Charles or a mention of a location so that I'd know something of the plan. Alain's voice was low and somewhat muffled, so when I heard a shout, I was startled enough to gasp involuntarily. Instantly realizing that if Alain heard it, the jig would be up.

'Why Alain had shouted?' Hearing nothing further, I realized that Alain must have ended the call. At that moment, the car slowed, then stopped, and I still didn't know where we were or what had caused Alain's loud reaction.

Relieved that he must not have heard my inopportune gasp, I waited to see what Alain would do next.

Are we at the place where we're meeting Charles or has Alain stopped for gas? I wondered. I decided to risk a peek from under the throw. Slowly I pulled back a corner of the throw and poked my head out. "Ahh!" There, looking down on me with that smug, yes, I'm sorry – French 'tude was Alain. And standing beside him was a man I'd never seen before. He was an older, very good-looking Frenchman with salt and pepper hair – and he was looking down at me with the same expression as Alain.

Forty minutes later - I was bound and gagged and sitting not very comfortably, in a confessional. The moment I saw Alain and the other Frenchman, I realized that I was on the wrong side of this adventure. Besides cursing me using words I figured they couldn't use in polite French society - the men hadn't uttered a word of explanation.

Instead, they hustled me back into my hiding place, and the good-looking one got in beside me and showed me his very impressive gun. I prudently decided to wait on asking any questions and instead buried my head deeper into the blanket.

Where could Charles be? – It seemed that Alain's loyalty to his employer didn't extend to protecting his lady friend.

Now here I was in a confessional in a church I'd never seen before, being guarded by a rogue agent and his *unfortunately* very handsome associate. *What was it about Frenchmen?*

Clearly, I have a weakness for them, I thought.

Time passed, and I wondered what was happening. From what I gathered Alain hadn't told Charles that he didn't share his viewpoint on ending this crime spree. Clearly, Alain had aligned himself with the group who were now winning - the ones that had stolen the Hassam years ago, attacked me on the street, days ago and who had lured Charles away from me hours ago. In my naïve way, I'd always thought of criminals as parasites, similar to spammers - People who will go out of their way to take from someone else and who will hurt and kill for pleasure were the worst of the worst. They preyed on others and were the lowest of the low, in my opinion.

I mused about what I'd do to them if it were up to me and then realized that I was in a church and in fact, in a confessional, having these uncharitable thoughts about fellow human beings, and I was ashamed. As an act of penance, I said three 'Our Fathers.'

CHAPTER 40

Charles found himself with a couple of hours to kill before he had to get to St Eustace. He was planning to make his way there during rush hour, as Parisians returned home from work, figuring he wouldn't be noticed amidst the market stalls and the crowds coming from the Metro if Marco was surveilling.

He decided to go home for a few hours. He could do with a shower, and he was looking forward to calling the Mont and finding out what Ellen had done with her day.

"Allo? Charles recognized Bertrand's voice answering the phone. He was momentarily surprised that Alain hadn't answered, but he wasn't concerned. "Georges! How are the ladies doing? Has Ellen been trying to get you to let her get into the private parts of the Abbey? I fully expected when I called that you would be tendering your resignation. Ellen can be a handful!"

"Non, mon Amie. She didn't come on the tour of the Mont today – she chose to stay behind. And when we got back, she was napping. So, I haven't seen her since shortly after you left this morning. Cathy intends to wake her up in a few minutes so that we can plan dinner. With Alain gone, I decided we'd take the women to dinner in town. Louis and Jacque and I can handle the three women."

"Where is Alain?" Charles asked with a bit of an edge.

"Alain told us you had called him to Paris to help you," Bertrand explained feeling a sense of dread. Charles was always so calm and measured in conversation. The tightness in his voice warned Bertrand that something wasn't right, and Charles' next sentence confirmed that.

"I did not! And I am getting a bad feeling about this. Send Cathy upstairs right away to check on Ellen – I'll wait!"

Charles could feel his heartbeat racing. He was processing this new information and wondering if he could get to the Mont and back before the meet with Marco.

"She's not 'ere!" Bertrand's voice pitch had a hint of panic in it.

"Think," Charles demanded. "When was the last time you saw her?"

"We saw her just before we left to tour the Mont. Ellen decided that she was still tired and wanted to have a quiet morning. About 11:30, Alain called and said that he'd been called to join you in Paris, and he requested we come back here and get Ellen. As soon as we arrived, he hopped into the car and explained that Ellen was napping. That was at Noon." Bertrand explained.

"Noon? It's four o'clock" Do you mean to say that in 4 hours, not one of you – even her Aunt wasn't curious about why she was sleeping so long?" Charles was terrified! Ellen and trouble seemed to be intimately involved. He began to think about what Bertrand had said.

"You said that Alain wanted you to come back here for Ellen?"

"Yes, he said you had asked him to join you and that since he couldn't leave Ellen alone, we would have to come back here and get her."

"So, unfortunately, it seems that Ellen joined Alain – Alain didn't take Ellen. Merde! That woman promised me that she'd behave and wait for me there and the moment I turn my back, she's inserted herself back into the crime. I wouldn't be surprised if she's hidden in the back seat of Alain's car at this very moment. Find Alain – we'll find Ellen."

Bertrand couldn't have felt worse, and he told Charles so. "Charles – I can't imagine how she did it. The only time she wasn't with us, she was with Alain. How could she have slipped away without him noticing?"

"That WOMAN would cause an agnostic to call for a priest! She is perhaps the sneakiest person I've ever encountered and considering that I'm a cop, you can imagine I've met some pretty sneaky criminals."

Charles was beside himself, and his ordinarily calm reserve had disappeared. He had no idea what Ellen had gotten herself involved in. What could Alain have been doing? Why would he have lied about meeting me? Then a thought occurred to him.

"Bertrand – did Alain take the limo?"

"Yes, he did. I thought since he was meeting you, you'd asked him to bring it."

"In my study on my laptop is a GPS program. I've recently added a tracker to the limo and haven't had a chance to tell Alain about it. Go into the study and start up the laptop. Then I'll tell you what to do."

"Yes, boss, right away!" Charles could hear Bertrand hustle through the foyer, and he could hear concerned questions coming from Cathy and Eleanor. Bertrand calmly put them off, and momentarily he came back onto the line. For a few minutes, Charles relayed technical commands and instructions, and when he finished, they had Alain's exact coordinates.

Charles couldn't be more surprised. At that very moment, the Limo, apparently carrying Alain and Ellen was parked on a side street beside St. Eustace.

CHAPTER 41

My perch in the confessional was initially comfortable, but as time passed, I began to feel my butt deaden. I readjusted and shifted but couldn't manage to get comfortable and wondered from time to time if Alain and his handsome but dangerous friend were still guarding me, but as if sensing my curiosity, they'd begin talking.

After what must have been two or three hours, I realized I had a very urgent need to answer natures' call and wondered if they'd allow me that freedom.

"Alain, please!   I need to go to the bathroom. I'm very much afraid if you don't let me, I will end up defiling this ancient confessional! I can't imagine how many rosaries that will cost me!"

I was hoping that my plea reached Alain, who let's face it hadn't proven to be overly concerned about my welfare – definitely not a fan!

"Alright come with me – there's nobody 'ere right now, but any action from you to escape will guarantee you consequences." Alain's tone confirmed what I'd feared -- he didn't feel any compassion or responsibility for me. He'd joined the dark side.

The petulant Frenchman lead me down one of the aisles and to a public restroom, which judging from its appearance probably hadn't been seen to since the church opened.

As tempted as I was to be safe again, I had no intention of escaping at that point. I knew for sure now that the man Alain was with, was Marco and if I just bided my time for a bit, my captors would meet up with the long arm of French justice — in the form of Charles.

CHAPTER 42

After realizing that Ellen was close by and in danger – certainly, Alain had found her by now – Charles ordered Bertrand to pack up the ladies and take them to the Ritz. He would keep them secure there since Alain must have told Marco they were on the Mont today.

He hung up with Bertrand and phoned Boutin, who was not happy to be woken from his sleep but agreed that he would meet Charles in the Les Halles cafe - Le Chien qui Fume' and go from there to Les Halles and St. Eustache. Charles knew that Marco and Alain were likely to have lookouts and to be there early. Charles needed to find out what was going on in St. Eustache without being seen. He couldn't go himself because Alain and Marco both knew him by sight. Chances are they knew Boutin as well, so Charles contacted Georges who had looked after Ellen a few nights earlier and explained what he needed.

Georges was eager to help and agreed to wander through St. Eustace with his digital camera and take some 'pics' – 'if we're lucky he will see or photograph exactly where Alain and Marco are,' Charles thought to himself.

Once Georges had 'toured' the church and plaza in front, he would meet Boutin and Charles at the cafe, and they'd review the pictures.

CHAPTER 43

Alain managed to get Ellen back from the restroom without incident – a fact which surprised him. The newly docile Ellen kept her word and never tried to escape. *she knows I would hurt her if she tried – I've scared her; now she'll cooperate.* he thought to himself.

Back at the confessional, he and Marco hiding in the shadows, the church was beginning to fill with tourists pausing to light candles and take photographs in the dimming interior.

These tourists, he thought to himself, act as if everything is a famous monument. One man was walking about photog-raphing every corner in the place. Alain was instantly nervous that he and Marco would end up on his film role. But fortunately, they were sufficiently in the shadows to ensure that their faces were hidden.

Marco himself was kneeling with his head down as if in prayer, until the tourist dropped a guide book on the floor. As he leaned down to pick it up, Marco's head swiveled up, quickly returning to his prayerful pose.

Alain surreptitiously rechecked his watch. 6:30 pm. They weren't waiting until 10 pm for Albert. Marco knew that was not a possibility now that Ellen was with them. He'd left a message with Albert's roommate in a code they'd planned earlier – "Tell Albert, that the concert has been res-cheduled to nine pm. He should arrive early to ensure himself a seat."

Now all they had to do was wait. Albert, who had turned out to be an enthusiastic employee, was sure to be there by eight or eight-thirty. By then, the church, which closed at seven, would be empty, and they could meet in peace.

CHAPTER 44

George was happy to help out his friend Charles. He knew that solving this case was important to him but seeing how he behaved with Ellen a few days earlier, he also recognized that Charles had finally fallen in love again.

Charles had been alone a long time, his marriage to Isabelle ending in tragedy soon after it began. They'd been on their honeymoon in Turkey when a bomb detonated in a street market. Charles had drifted away from Isabelle's side to look at rugs in a stall nearby. When he'd heard the explosion, he momentarily froze, then took off running to get to her. It was too late. Part of a wall crushed her. There was nothing he could do for her. She died while he held her hand – the only part of her he could touch.

George knew a different Charles after that. No longer the lively young man he'd known at university. Charles had become very serious, very focused on his job. Now, fifteen years later, George was noticing a spark in Charles' eyes and a lighter spirit. Ellen had done that for Charles, now George had to make sure that this relationship didn't end in tragedy also.

He mused about the difference in Charles as he wandered around the interior of the church, taking hundreds of pictures along the way. He had realized that unless he took many pictures, it might look suspicious to the bad guys when he got to them. He also jostled a guide book in his hand, hoping it made the tourist cover more authentic.

At one point he'd reached the left corner at the back of the church and saw two men presumably praying in a pew outside a confessional. One man stared forward, the other - his head down in submission. There was something about the man who was facing forward – he seemed to be very attuned to Georges' movements. George spent a few minutes in the area – taking numerous pictures of the statues and woodwork. He could feel the man's eyes on his back and knew he had found what he was looking for.

Georges had to be sure though that he had a photo of the other man. So, acting clumsily, he dropped the guide book on the floor and pretended to struggle with the camera as the man looked up. He held his finger on the camera button, shooting away sans flash as he slowly leaned down to get the fallen book. With a whispered apology for interrupting their prayer, George beat feet for the door.

CHAPTER 45

Back at the cafe, Charles and Boutin quietly planned how they would capture Alain, and with any luck, Marco.

Charles was relieved to see Georges when he finally arrived at the cafe. He was ebullient, proclaiming, "I've got a picture of your two bad guys!"

Charles anxiously asked, "any sign of Ellen?"

"No, but I suspect I know where they are keeping her," Georges answered.

George went through the digital pictures until he came to one of the two suspicious men – one staring and one praying. "You see – this is them!" George said proudly.

"Merde! That is Alain – and though I can't see his face, I am certain that is Marco." Charles declared.

"Here is one of the praying man's face!" George offered.

"Yes – as I suspected it is Marco. Well done, Georges – we'll have to make you an honorary flic." Charles praised Georges.

"You see the confessional behind them – I think that is where they must have Ellen," Georges explained.

The three spent a few minutes going over the details and layout of the church and where exactly Alain and Marco were in it. By the time they finished, it was 7:30 and Charles knew that he had to get into the church.

Being a cop had its' advantages. He knew the church would have closed at seven so getting in now would take some work, but he knew the organist who worked there, and he asked him to meet him at the church with his keys and a hat. Charles would go in disguised as the organist and, hopefully, wrap this up tonight.

CHAPTER 46

I had long since tired of waiting for rescue in the confessional. It was dark and smelled of hundreds of years of incense which had worked its way into the grains of the wood that cradled me. My captors had kindly not restrained my arms, but my feet were tied together, not too professionally, with a long piece rope Alain had brought from the car. It took me all of 30 seconds to dispose of that ill-administered binding, and I was free. Let's face it, the main reason I was sitting here was not because I was immobilized, but because of the two men who sat just outside.

I sat and contemplated my situation. As time passed, the plan to do nothing and wait for Charles was beginning to wane.
Logically, I knew I couldn't overwhelm the two men – they were much bigger, and they each had two good arms, and I also knew that it could be hours before Charles showed up – if at all. It was that last part that scared me. What if Charles didn't know there was something about to go down here in the church?

So, I have no one to rely on but myself.

Could I make enough of a nuisance of myself that perhaps they'd leave me behind? I wasn't sure, but I knew I'd tested Charles' patience before, and he had a crush on me. But these were wily criminals. Would they get irritated enough to leave me, or would I push them into a more violent act?

I also had no means of protecting myself. All I had with me was a pocketbook, and there was nothing that could be considered a weapon in there: no nail file or set of keys. My wallet was pretty heavy, but I doubted that I could injure my captors by clocking them with it.

Then I flashed on the other contents – hair spray, cosmetics and *Oh, My GOD! Painkillers!*

I had my painkillers in there and would indeed have loved one or two for myself, but even more importantly, to save myself.

Alain had brought along a thermos of coffee - an indication that he was planning for a long night.

Perfect! – drop several into the thermos and then pretty soon – Bon Nuit Alain and Hot-French Guy! I thought, feeling hopeful all of a sudden.

It's something! With great effort to avoid any noise, I slipped several pain-killers out of the bottle and palmed them.

"Alain – pssst! Alain?"

"What—be quiet, or I'll gag you!"

"I'm sorry, but I'm so thirsty – is there any way I can get a bit of your coffee?"

Alain threw me a withering look and handed the thermos over.

Carefully, to avoid dropping the pills, I opened the top of the thermos, poured a small amount into the cup for me and dropped the pills into the thermos.

I made appreciative noises over the coffee and handed the closed thermos back to Alain after giving it a little shake.

"Thanks, that was very helpful of you," I said gratefully. Little did they know how helpful it would prove to be.

The church was getting cold, and I wondered what they were waiting for. I knew that they were here to meet someone, but when? And how soon before they drank the coffee and nodded off?

Like an answer to the prayers I'd been making in the quiet of my confessional, Alain took the thermos and offered some to his friend. The hot Frenchman took a long drink, then another and handed it back to Alain. Alain threw a dark look at his friend, obviously mad at how much the other had drunk and poured the rest down his throat.

Hee hee hee! My evil plan may work! I celebrated silently.

CHAPTER 47

"Charles, everyone is in place. Your friend Msr. Milot is waiting for you in the courtyard behind the giant head." Boutin said.

"Ok – what we don't know for sure is if a hand-off is planned. We don't want to miss our opportunity to get the paintings back, but we need to get Ellen out to safety as a priority. If we do things right, we'll be able to do both. Let's go!"

Charles and his team moved out through the darkened Les Halles park. Although beautiful during the day, at night, this area harbored the less attractive element of Paris; the drug addicts and dealers; prostitutes and unfortunates.

Not an area that most of Parisian society would be flocking to tonight and Charles was happy about that. He had often said that his line of work was not dangerous, but this case had proven him wrong on several occasions.

He tried to dismiss his worry about how Ellen was faring and couldn't. On the one hand, he was angrier than ever at her for putting herself in harm's way – again. But on the other hand, he admired her determination to be her own person and follow her own will. Those two qualities were the things that attracted Charles to her in the first place. Of course, she was lovely, and that spirit of hers came pouring out the moment she flashed the first smile at him.

As Charles approached the front of St. Eustache, he saw his acquaintance, Msr. Milot and approached him, thanking him for his help.

"Ce n'est rien," said Milot.

"Well, it isn't nothing. This is an important break in our case. Merci," Charles replied.

Charles took the keys and the hat from Msr. Milot and joined his team. Charles would be entering from the rear approach as Milot had told him he would enter, every night. So, if Alain and Marco had been observing the comings and goings at the church, everything would look normal.

Boutin would cover the rear entrance, and two detectives would enter as Charles did so that one door closing is all that their targets would hear.

Fortunately, the rear entrance was in the corner of the building that Georges had identified as the location where he believed they were holding Ellen.

He was whistling, as Msr. Milot had told him he usually did. Charles and his team approached the rear entrance and with guns drawn opened the door.

As he entered the darkened church anteroom, Charles' eyes darted from side to side. The two detectives with him stayed out of sight, and Charles tucked the gun in the waist of his pants and began his walk to the organ at the left rear of the church. With his hat pulled down low and with an overcoat hanging on his shoulders, Charles knew that Marco and Alain would not recognize him. He had seen two figures on the left of the entrance but not Ellen. He'd also seen the confessional beside where the two men sat and agreed with Georges that that was Ellen's location.

His plan with his team was to appear to be walking to the organ and pretend at the last moment that he noticed the two men. He'd politely and with some surprise question them about why they were there after closing and give his detectives the distraction they needed to enter unnoticed.

Charles opened his mouth to speak, but he was beaten to it by Alain. "Hey, old man, no organ practice tonight. Au Revoir." Alain said with menace in his voice.

"Pardon?" Answered Charles. "Of course, I'm practicing tonight -I do every night. And do you realize the church is closed?"

"We have permission to be here, but you should leave if you know what's good for you," Alain said his voice beginning to lose definition and slur a bit. Marco, beside him, hadn't raised his head and Alain was afraid he'd fallen asleep.

At that moment, when Ellen heard the discussion in the church, she knew without a doubt that the 'old man' was Charles and her rescue was imminent.

Charles slowly approached the two men. He didn't want it to appear deliberate, but as if he was approaching to finish his conversation with Alain.

Alain, though his reflexes were slowing down, was attuned to his surroundings by his training in the military. There was something bold about the older man and something familiar. He jabbed Marco in the ribs, hoping for a reaction, and his boss turned his head slightly to the side, giving a 'go' glance to Alain.

That was all Alain needed. He and Marco both knew the old man posed a threat.

With a quick but surreptitious movement, Alain had his gun drawn and pointed at Charles.

"Hey, Old Man – stop there, get on your knees and kiss the floor!" Alain snarled.

Ellen hearing from the confessional realized the pills hadn't quite kicked in – just 15 more minutes and maybe Charles would be safe, but now he was a captive too!

Charles was not entirely surprised that Alain found his 'old man' character threatening. He had hired Alain for his military training and instincts, although those skills were now being used against him.

Charles plotted his next move. He knew that the detectives that came in with him were somewhere close by, and he was sure that they had heard Alain's outburst. From his position on the floor, Charles couldn't reach his gun inside his coat, but if he could distract Alain for a moment, perhaps he could.

At that moment, he was aware of movement behind the two men. He cursed under his breath because he knew the source of the movement. Ellen to the rescue! He had to do something quickly before Ellen put herself in danger.

CHAPTER 48

Now that my legs were free, and Charles was near, I felt encouraged to open the door to the confessional silently. Both men had their backs to me, and stupid Alain had left the thermos on the pew beside him like he was gifting me with my very own weapon.

I planned to clock Alain with it and while Hot French Guy was distracted, wipe the smile off HIS face.

From my perch at the door of the confessional, I struggled to translate the conversation between Alain and Charles. My rudimentary knowledge of the language wasn't helpful. Instinct took over, however when I realized their earnestness and the threatening tone in Alain's voice. When Alain produced a gun, I knew I had to try something!

My childhood hours watching the Three Stooges -- Larry, Moe, and Curley provided me with just the answer I needed!

Without any hesitation or fear of failure, I grabbed the Thermos with my right hand, tip-toed up behind my two captors, planted my feet firmly on the ground and swung the thermos from left to right with all my strength.

Hot French Guy was the first to react, screaming and cupping his now bleeding right ear. Alain, slowed down by the piggish amount of doped up coffee he'd drunk, listed to the left, and dropped his gun.

That gave the two detectives with Charles, and Charles himself, time to shift the dynamic to one of power.

Charles grabbed the gun and closed the distance between himself, Alain and Marco.

But, it was too late -Before I could say 'knuck, knuck, knuck! Hot French Guy had a gun at my temple.

Hot French Guy had rebounded from his injury long enough to reach one cashmere covered arm out and grab me by the collar. The gun he apparently had handy.

Charles realizing he'd lost 'hand' in the conflict, calmly said: "Listen, Marco, she has nothing to do with this -- let her go and you and I can settle things between the two of us."

Charles had telegraphed his willingness to deal by adopting a much less offensive posture. He held the gun by the grip under the trigger, and he motioned for his colleagues to back off.

So Hot French Guy is Marco, I thought, just in time to realize his grip on my collar had loosened. For a moment, it seemed as though he was considering Charles' offer -- until Marco jammed the barrel of the gun into my temple and started backing away.

"You know what I want, and so I will hold on to what you want until you're ready to deal."

Charles could see that Marco was serious, and he didn't want to do anything to antagonize him further. It was evident that he was willing to trade Ellen's life for a painting.

Charles had no intention of giving up either.

Alain, recovering from his humiliating decking by a girl, was standing now and clearly back in fighting form. Charles realizing this, felt he had no choice but to capitulate to Marco's demands.

Charles dropped his gun and nodded his assent to Marco. He tried to telegraph some courage to Ellen, but even though Ellen looked scared, he noted her posture was not defeated, and there was a glint of anger emanating from her eyes.

'She'll be fine until I can get her.' Charles thought to himself.

Marco dragged Ellen out of the church cave-man style.

CHAPTER 49

Charles knew he had to let Marco and Ellen go. He could see from Marco's demeanor there was no negotiating with him, but he did have one hope -- that Marco would use the limo that Alain had driven into Paris. Perhaps the GPS would lead Charles to Marco's next destination.

The moment Marco disappeared from view with Alain and Ellen, Charles and his men ran for the front exit. He was just in time to note the limo disappearing from view. His delight, however, abruptly disappeared when he reached the street and found the GPS unit crushed as if it had been driven over.

Frustrated and more scared than he'd ever been in his life, Charles began barking orders to the cops accompanying him.

Boutin, was nowhere in sight and just as Charles was hoping his friend had managed to follow the car, his cell phone vibrated. He'd barely answered it with a clipped "Oui!" when he was interrupted by the brusque voice of his friend.

"Boutin here -- the limo is heading towards the Eiffel Tower."

"You managed to follow it? Mon Dieu, you're good!" Charles' fear instantly turned to delight on hearing this news from Boutin. In the next moment, his elation disappeared as his old friend imparted some important news..."

"I am with them, taken at the back of the church. It seems that Marco has a new boss -- one that's not afraid to use violent means. Alain is running the show now. Ellen and I are in the back of the limo, and I'm only allowed to call you to tell you what I have and that if you don't let him leave the country, he will push Ellen and myself off the top of the Eiffel Tower."

"How is it that he is allowing you to tell me this now? Is there something else I don't know -- cough twice if they've told you what to say?" Charles, pacing and dragging hard on a Gitane, listened carefully for the signal -- and there it was. Two throaty coughs from Boutin.

"Do you have a weapon? Cough once for yes and snort for no." A snort answered the question definitively.

How about your cell -- I can find your position with your cell. Do you have it? -- answer yes or no. Make something up..."

"Yes, my friend -- I'm afraid it's true. Alain is not afraid to kill --"

With that, the connection was cut, and Charles was left standing in the courtyard of St. Eustache staring at the phone in his hand and praying that he could trace their location.

CHAPTER 50

With just three words from Charles, "Find them NOW!" the courtyard of St. Eustache erupted into chaos. The detectives who'd been in the church with him were directing the multiple flics who'd responded when Charles came out of the church. Each detective took a team and were given orders to follow different leads.

Lt. Montaigne was taking three flics to the Eiffel Tower on the off chance that Alain was actually heading there. Montaigne had already called and ordered the monument closed.

Lt. LaMotte and two more senior patrolmen were going to the Mont to search Alain's belongings, even though Charles knew Alain was smart enough not to leave anything behind to incriminate himself.

Charles and Bertrand, who by now had returned from the Mont after stashing the ladies at the Ritz (a hotel whose security was assured) were working together to trace the GPS signal from Boutin's phone. Bertrand had a brilliant idea - to station a police car at various busy intersections so that if they got a signal, they could transmit it to the car at the closest location and follow the limo from there.

The problem now was that they weren't getting any signal. When Charles had initially connected to Boutin's signal, there was an indication that the limo was going in the direction of the Tour Eiffel, but then, it abruptly dropped from sight.

CHAPTER 51

Boutin hoped that Ellen wouldn't cause any more drama, but from the look of her, the fight had gone. She was leaning against the glass of the limo window with a faraway look in her eyes, her good shoulder -- the one nearest him, drooped in submission. He was afraid to talk to her because their captors were quite attentive. He feared that any word, however benign would raise their suspicions and that they may be separated. He knew now that his priority would be to keep Ellen safe until Charles was able to find them.

He had no doubts about Charles' ability to do so. Charles had proven time and time again that his instincts were sharp and his nose for the right path to take was acute.

* * * * * * * *

Initially, on leaving the church, I had a spark of courage, but we'd been driving around for some time, and the adrenaline I had at first had subsided. My taste for the fight had left me. Tired as I was, I now wanted this entire nightmare to be over. Seeing a gun pointed at Charles, and my current role as a hostage had subdued me.

This time I knew that I wasn't entirely responsible for the situation I was in. Ultimately Alain and Marco were to blame for that. But I had crawled into the limo back at Mont Saint Michel and so, compromised my own safety.

Now I want it all to be over. I want to see Paris from a Seine boat, I want to climb the Eiffel Tower and pose for a picture on top (and not to be thrown off of it), and I want very much to kiss Charles in the moonlight on a Quai on the banks of the Seine, I thought.

CHAPTER 52

The limo seemed to be driving in circles. Boutin had seen the I. M. Pei pyramid three times already, and he wondered why. It felt as if Alain and Marco were waiting for something. They'd been driving now for 45 minutes and were still within a mile of the Church, where they'd been taken.

Marco'd taken his phone when he was captured but had given it to him to call Charles. As soon as the call ended, however, he was forced to give it back. Alain had made a show of turning it off and sneered "we don't want the GPS to give us away -- do we?" So, tracking them by his phone was out of the question now.

Their endless circles of Paris' first arrondissement were wearing on Boutin's nerve. The thing that worried him was that they seemed almost to be waiting to be discovered by Charles' men. Staying in so close to the site of the kidnapping seemed risky, and although he was grateful for Alain's seeming carelessness, Boutin worried that something else was afoot.

At that moment, Boutin became aware that the limo was stopping. He glanced out the window and noted they were alongside the Seine and there was a bateau-mouche directly below.

Alain jumped out of the front of the limo and swiftly pulled open Ellen's door, very nearly dumping her out onto the street. She appeared dazed and alarmed, and Boutin realized that she must have dozed off in the last few minutes. Alain grabbed her by her good arm and jerked her upright. Ellen yelped in pain.

"Cochon!" Boutin barked. "She is injured! Be careful. Any further injury to the Americaine and Charles will kill you like the dog you are, once he captures you."

"Blanchard will not capture me! As long as he provides what he's been asked to provide, you will go free, and he'll be so happy to see you and his petite Amie, that he won't question your condition. On the other hand, if Blanchard does not come thru you, both will be dead, and we will be gone." Alain's arrogance and fierceness alarmed Boutin.

"Now -- get on the boat!" Alain gave a push to Ellen to start her down the stairs to the boat. Boutin scrambled out after her, noting that Marco was still sitting quietly in the limo. There was no one else about, and Boutin briefly considered attacking the younger man, but not knowing if Marco was armed, discarded the plan. He obediently followed behind Ellen, with a gun at his back.

At the bottom of the stairs, Boutin reached out to Ellen and placed his hand reassuringly on her shoulder, which he could feel trembling.

As they approached the boat, it seemed that there was no one on board. Boutin knew that this was the opportunity he'd waited for to make something happen. Marco was still up in the car, and so it was just he and Ellen and Alain.

With a swift shove, Boutin pushed Ellen aside -- hoping she'd land on her uninjured shoulder -- and he kicked to the left, unbalancing Alain. Alain, surprised, dropped the gun, which Boutin kicked out of the way with his now descending foot. As he jammed his shoulder into Alain's solar plexus, Alain recovered himself long enough to land a roundhouse punch to Boutin's chin. Momentarily stunned Boutin lost his balance and began to fall. Alain took advantage of that stumble and rounded on him again. The two men grappled together on the quai, and each gained and lost advantage time and time again.

Ellen, unnoticed during the struggle had gotten to her feet and was making her way around the fighting men to where the gun had landed. Moving slowly so as not to be detected, she made her way to the gun. And then she was there! Reaching down, she grabbed the gun, which felt so heavy in her inexperienced hands. Pointing it now she mustered her strength, pointed the gun in the air, and pulled the trigger.

The sharp report of the gunshot stunned the combatants -- but Alain was faster, and he reached into his pant leg to retrieve his other gun -- it was gone! It was lost during his struggle with Boutin. Rising up slowly, he glanced around him on the ground and said, "put the gun down mademoiselle -- you don't know what you're doing." To prove him wrong, Ellen squeezed off another round, this one more in the vicinity of his feet. As Alain hopped about and spun around, he came face to face with Boutin, who was holding what Alain recognized as his spare gun.

Boutin couldn't help but smile as the realization of his situation spread across Alain's face.

Alain, not so graciously, raised his hands in an international gesture of surrender.

"Nicely done Ellen!" Boutin commended her - both relieved and impressed.

"Well," Ellen said, "that's not something I'd ever imagined in my life, that I could do. Now I'll give it to you for safe-keeping." and she handed it by the barrel to Boutin.

"Why not just give it to me my dear - "a voice behind Ellen purred.

CHAPTER 53

Charles was at his wit's end. It had been more than 3 hours since the limo carrying Ellen and Boutin disappeared from GPS. Charles had stationed men at intersections around Paris, and another contingent, at various junctures in the Eiffel Tower, and they hadn't a single lead to follow.

Charles knew that Alain was dangerous, and he wondered if Marco was being used as a pawn. What he truly feared more than anything else was that Ellen would try to take matters into her own hands, putting her life at risk. His one hope was that Boutin -- the most natural cop he'd ever worked with would come up with some way of protecting Ellen and bringing this kidnapping to an end.

His staff of detectives was at work, back at headquarters, trying to get some information on Alain and how he was connected to Marco. Charles blamed himself for hiring Alain as a bodyguard. He'd done a background check on him but acknowledged to himself that he was so impressed with Alain's military background that he didn't look too hard.

He knew that Alain was an only child of a wealthy elderly Parisian couple - most likely adopted, for records of his birth were unavailable. Despite being raised as a privileged son, Alain had worked hard in school and joined the French military at 18.

His parents were now dead -- his mother had died most recently, two years ago. Charles remembered that Alain had gone to the funeral, but he hadn't arranged it; something that Charles never thought to ask about. Who would have arranged it in his place? And, there was never any talk of an inheritance. Surely, coming from such wealth, Alain would have benefitted after his parents' death. Alain just kept on working for Charles and living a very modest life. He seemingly had no friends and kept no social life. There weren't women (or men for that matter).

Twenty-four hours ago, Charles would have sworn to Alain's loyalty 100%, and sadly, never saw this betrayal coming. *What led him to turn on Charles? Where had he taken Ellen and Boutin?*

Charles hoped that his staff came up with answers to these questions.

CHAPTER 54

At the Ritz, Cathy and Eleanor waited anxiously for word of Ellen. Since they'd been hustled here by Bertrand, the two women had paced and waited in silence for the word of her safe return. Bertrand had said nothing to them about what had happened, only that Ellen and Charles were involved in some element of the case.

Bertrand had placed a stout female cop in their suite with them. He wasn't taking any further chances. The elevators had been locked out of their floor and the stairwell doors locked as well.

To Eleanor and Cathy, it almost seemed like they were prisoners again, but the difference this time was that they were safe.

To make the time go by Cathy and Eleanor read magazines and books that had kindly been provided by the hotel.

CHAPTER 55

Having celebrated our freedom too soon, Boutin and I surrendered to Marco, who had been made wise to our escape attempt from the gunshots I'd squeezed off.

Now, the two of us were in the hold of the waiting bateau-mouche, sailing down the Seine. Since the windowless room was secure, Marco and a limping Alain did not cuff us, and I was grateful for that. Boutin's attempt to get me out of harm's way had jammed my good shoulder, and the bad one continued to ache. I had a graze on the right side of my forehead, also as a result of my fall. That was bleeding earlier but had stopped and crusted over now. Even without a mirror, I knew I must look like a mess, but my body ached so much now, I couldn't afford the effort to 'tidy up.'

Boutin was sitting on the edge of a chair assessing the damage to himself. His jaw throbbed, and both top and bottom lips were swelling. There was a sharp pain in the area of his ribs, and the knuckles on his right hand were raw and bleeding. The worst pain he felt, however, was the sting of failure. He'd had Alain stopped but had forgotten about the threat of Marco.

"Mademoiselle, I am very sorry that I allowed Marco to capture us again! I was so caught up in the heat of the moment, scrambling about on the ground with Alain, that I didn't think about Marco being up in the car! I could have ended this abduction, and I failed! Je Suis desolee! And since we surrendered to Marco, they have the other gun too."

"But I'm the one thoughtless enough to have fired the gun!" I exclaimed. "I didn't need to shoot the gun off -- I guess I've seen too many cops and robbers shows. I should have just threatened him with it. The fact that

Marco heard gunshots is what lead us here." I explained with a voice weary with defeat.

"Mademoiselle, I know you feel guilty, but that was a courageous thing you did, and even if it didn't work out for us, Charles would have been as proud of you, as am I. Let's not focus on that now. We have to come up with a plan to get out of here. You heard me tell Charles what they've planned for us. We cannot let that happen."

The kindly tone of his voice struck me, and it almost made me feel better. I was confident in Boutin's skills, and I knew I had to shake off the specter of what had just happened on the Quai.

"What do you have in mind, Lieutenant?"

CHAPTER 56

Charles had given up waiting to hear reports from his staff in the field. As he drove himself back to police headquarters, he thought about what options he had available.

This was not a routine theft -- not with Alain now involved. Marco has moved into more significant and more dangerous territory.

Passing over the Pont Neuf, he noticed what a beautiful night it was in Paris. He had always felt a thrill of gratitude that this was his home. Nowhere in the world did he feel the catch in his breath as he did at a moment like this -- the Eiffel Tower was blinking in the distance and below on the Seine, a bateau-mouche quietly passed out of sight under the span.

He wished he could share this moment with Ellen. He wanted to pose for a picture with her on top of the Eiffel Tower, and he wanted very much to kiss her in the moonlight on a Quai on the banks of the Seine.

None of that would happen, he realized, unless he found them. He had to get a break in this case!

The fact that Marco was still expecting to make an exchange for the Renoir and guaranteed safe passage from France was reassuring but also confusing. For it seemed that he didn't know he had both. Someone else had a hand in what was happening – someone Alain represented, and that person was keeping Marco around as Suspect #1.

At least Charles knew that he had one sure way to see Ellen again. An appoint-ment on the top of the Eiffel Tower was a risk, but it was what Marco and Alain were expecting and what Charles now must deliver if he were ever to see Ellen again.

CHAPTER 57

Boutin had several ideas for escaping the bateau-mouche, but all of them involved jumping into the chilly Seine, and he was concerned that Ellen, with her injured arm, would not be able to swim. When he discussed his plan with Ellen, however, she explained to him that if it meant escaping, she would risk it. But Boutin wasn't sure. Charles was counting on him to protect Ellen. And how was he protecting her by allowing such a thing to happen?

What he was thinking about now was trying to slip off the boat on his own hoping they wouldn't notice. If he had fifteen minutes to get to dry land and to a phone, he could possibly be back in time to capture Alain and Marco before they knew he was gone.

Then Ellen would be safe, and this crime wave would be at an end.

"Lieutenant, why don't we start by telling them I have to use the bathroom. They already let me go once, but that was hours ago in the church. Surely, they will respond to that, it will get them to open the door of this room, and perhaps we can seize an opportunity then. After the beating you gave Alain, his reaction time is probably off. You could take him easily -- I'm certain of it! The only problem will be if Marco accompanies Alain -"

"Or if Marco comes himself --" Boutin interrupted. He is in much better condition right now. He'll put up a fight! And we know he has at least one gun -- I hesitate to risk it." Boutin sounded torn.

I got up and paced. Come to think of it the ruse wasn't much of a ruse. I was actually in need of a bathroom, and as I paced, became aware of just how hungry I was. The last thing I'd eaten was as my sunrise breakfast with Charles. I thought, wishing I could turn back time.

"That's it -- we tell them we're hungry and when they bring us food, we'll tell them I need the bathroom -- which I do. Marco or Alain will arrive with a tray, and while they're distracted settling things we'll knock them over the head, lock them in here and escape!"

Boutin had to smile. The plan was naively simple, but as he thought about it, it had some promise.

"We can but try." Boutin rose now with purpose. "Let's see what we can find for weapons."

We began to comb the room thoroughly. The more we looked, however, the lower our spirits became.

The filthy storage room was filled with crates and boxes -- some open. A quick perusal of their contents revealed cham-pagne and other liquor, miscellaneous cleaning supplies, linens and tins of caviar.

Clearly, this was a party boat. As I peeked in box after box, I tried to imagine using any of those things as a weapon. As carefully as I was paying attention, I nearly missed the perfect item - until I tripped over it. The long narrow box was partially hidden under the eaves of the boat, and my foot had kicked an edge of it up. There for all the wonder of it, was a rolled-up piece of canvas. My breath caught in my throat as I carefully drew the aged, stiff canvas gently out of the box.

"Boutin -- help me with this," I hissed, conscious of making too much noise.

Boutin came to my side and seeing what I had in my hands, passed an awestruck look at me as he gently took the two edges closest to him. As the two of us carefully unrolled the canvas, we realized we had our weapon.

After some whispered conversation, Boutin reverently entrusted the canvas to me and uttered "D'accord." moving to the door but pausing long enough to remove something from one of the open boxes.

He banged on the door, hoping only Marco would respond. Moments later, he heard footsteps coming down the corridor. Gratefully, he realized that they were normal, steady footsteps, not the halting footsteps of a man with a newly acquired limp.

As we waited for the door to open, we each looked to the other to ensure that we were ready for what was to happen next.

As the key jiggled in the lock, I moved into position; the canvas stretched out in front of me. Boutin equally seriously, removed the top from the bottle he was holding, making sure that the other bottle slung over his belt loop was also ready to go.

"What do you want mon amies?" Marco growled as he entered the room.

"What I don't want is to damage this precious Hassam painting with a bottle of excellent vintage champagne," Boutin murmured, as he wildly shook the bottle. "But I will do it if you don't follow my orders." Marco looked tensely from one to the other of them, calculating their intent. He could see that Boutin was fully prepared to spray the liquor on the painting that the Americaine was holding no more than five feet away.

As Marco grabbed for the painting, Boutin swung the bottle of bubbly liquid toward Marco connecting with his white smile. A sound of teeth breaking was followed by a curse, and the familiar smell of Windex as Boutin swiftly grabbed the bottle hanging from his belt and aimed a full stream at Marco's eyes.

As Marco reached to cover his eyes, I, having placed the canvas safely away from the stream of liquids, reached over and withdrew Marco's gun from its place in the front of his trousers.

Boutin dropped his makeshift weapon and wrestled Marco quickly to the corner of the room, securing him with handcuffs that had conveniently been hanging out of Marco's back pocket.

Knowing he had to move quickly since Alain was surely on his way, Boutin took the gun from me and silently made his way out into the corridor. He tucked himself back against the wall as the sound of uneven footsteps made their way down the metal steps.

At the bottom, he heard Alain pause, likely seeing the door to the hold open, light spilling out. At that moment, Boutin withdrew his pistol and continued his progress down the corridor, pausing in a doorway.

Fortunately for the dark corner he had chosen to hide in, Alain never knew he was there. As he heard Alain's breathing coming upon him, he bided his time and at the ultimate last moment, struck -- struck Alain on the temple with the butt of the gun I'd taken from Marco! Alain went down like a bag of cement.

A few minutes later, Boutin had dragged Alain into the hold with Marco and collected Ellen.

Being short one pair of handcuffs wasn't a challenge for me. I dragged a linen tablecloth from one of the boxes wet it and twisted it into bindings that would take some time for Alain to remove. Also, realizing the broken bottle would provide a means for cutting the bindings, I scooped it up and handed it to Boutin who tossed it into the Seine.

As a parting shot, I picked up the newly found Childe Hassam canvas and offered to return it to the Louvre for them.

With that, Boutin ushered me out of the hold, closed it, and locked it. The French epithets and threats retreated as the two of us made our way along the side of the boat.

Up on deck Boutin and I quickly made our way to the front of the Bateau. We could still hear pounding and yelling, but it only made us move faster. Boutin knew of Alain's history in special forces and was sure he'd find a way out of the hold reasonably quickly.

Ellen, feeling better with every step, driven by adrenaline was first to the wheelhouse, although it may have been Boutin's innate sense of manners which compelled him even at such a time to allow her ahead of him.

In the wheelhouse, a quick inspection revealed that the onboard phone had been removed and although the engines were running, it appeared that a computer was driving the boat. Boutin cautioned me to step back, fearing my random pressing of buttons would work against us.

For my part, I was mystified by the numerous controls and was reluctant to try anything for the same reason. Even my mother admits that I'm not very technical, I reminded myself. Some things make more sense to boys.

With that, I withdrew and perched on one of the seats in the wheelhouse and gazed across the Seine. It was another lovely night in Paris, and she knew now that she still had a chance for that picture with Charles and that romantic dance on the Quai.

"Merde!" Boutin growled. He turned to me, anguish in his eyes and announced -- There is a timer on this boat -- it seems that the course is set and can't be changed. Like Autopilot on a plane -- you can't stop it, and I don't know where it is taking us!"

"Well -- it is a Seine boat -- perhaps it is set for the same course it takes the tourists on! Where are we now -- ok -- there's the d'Orsay, we're heading towards I'le de la cite. It's fairly narrow there. Perhaps we can manage to get off and swim to the shore."

Boutin grumbled. "Charles will have my head if you drown in the Seine. No -- there needs to be another solution."

"Look, Boutin -- Charles is not here now, and it is up to us to escape this. Given his choice, don't you think he'd rather we escape and to let him know where we are than to allow ourselves to be driven around all night by a pilotless bateau-mouche? Perhaps we can signal someone in a passing boat?"

"Of course, I've already thought of that -- look around you. There is no boat traffic now -- no pedestrian traffic whatsoever!" Boutin was frustrated, and I knew that if he were alone, he would have already jumped off the bateau-mouche and made his escape. I also understood his concerns about jumping into the Seine -- I couldn't make it alone to the shore with only one good arm. I knew what I had to do. But first I had to pee!

CHAPTER 58

Charles felt a vibration in his phone and pulled over by I'le de la cite and took the phone from his back pants pocket. He saw that he'd missed a call from Montaigne.

As he got out of the car to call Montaigne back, he once again noted the slow-moving bateau-mouche cruising along the Seine in front of him.

"Yes - Montaigne -- Blanchard 'ere! What's your status? "

"All is well at Le Tour Eiffel. Nothing out of the ordinary. The tower's been cleared, and the site security is aware of the situation. I have 4 men on each level and 8 at the perimeter. I will advise should something change."

"Bon! I hope we don't have to use all your men, but for the time being please remain at post."

"D'accord! Au revoir!"

As Montaigne signed off, Charles mused that even with every precaution taken, Alain and Marco would find a way to slip through.

His phone vibrated again, and Charles answered it immediately -- "Oui!"

"Bertrand here -- we've found the Limo!"

Charles sped away to the location -the Right Bank at Quai du Louvre (and ironically the name of the missing Hassam painting), where the limo had turned up. Bertrand had assured Charles that the limo was empty and that there did not seem to be signs of a struggle.

His thoughts were chaotic as he sped through the deserted streets of Paris -- *where were they now? Was Ellen safe?* And with a small chuckle -- *were they safe from Ellen?*

Charles screeched to a stop at the back of the abandoned limo. He observed that all four doors were open, and two technicians were combing over it. As he approached Bertrand, Charles felt the first signs of hope in hours.

"Sir -- they've found no sign of damages or blood. The engine wasn't warm when they first approached the car -- so it's been here a while. I have several men combing the area for anyone who may have seen something -- that's where the bad news comes in . . ." he trailed off.

"Bad news? What is it?"

Bertrand pulled himself to his full height and explained, "a gypsy on the lower Quai reports hearing a heavy scuffle followed by two gunshots in succession, about an hour ago. He said he believed there was a woman and three men involved. He didn't see them leave. I pressed him for more information, but that was all he had."

Charles' stomach lurched at the report of two gunshots -- *one for Ellen and one for Boutin?*, he worried.

"Did the witness report another car in the area? Did he see where they went? Where is this gypsy?" Charles peppered Bertrand with questions, all the while, feeling the acid fill his gut. He knew that the presence of gunshots had taken this situation to a new level. *Was Ellen shot? Boutin?* These questions rolled around in his brain as he followed Bertrand over to the bedraggled gypsy who'd given them the first information they'd had in hours.

Charles had to crank down his anxiety a bit before he spoke to the man, so he stepped aside and stood at the edge of the Seine and lit a cigarette. The river was still quiet. That lone bateau-mouche he'd seen earlier had disappeared from sight, and the river slept. Presently he felt his stomach settle, and as he put out his butt, he knew he could control his interrogation of the gypsy.

He walked back to where Bertrand stood beside the man on the bench, and as he neared him said: "What is your name?"

"Jean Cote, monsieur." The words were quiet and slurred.

"Un plaisir, monsieur. Please tell me what you saw." Charles asked in a subdued tone.

"I was sleeping on the wall over there when I awoke to the sounds of fighting. This often happens down here in the night, but when I looked, I noticed a woman fall and there were two men fighting."

"Two men? Are you sure there weren't three?" Charles interjected, curious about where the other man was.

"Non. There were just two then. The third one appeared after the woman fired the gun." Cote declared, stunning Charles and Bertrand.

"The woman had the gun?" Charles' heart leaped! It seemed that whenever he had written off Ellen as a 'victim,' she managed to pull out a surprise. Ellen and Boutin weren't shot - Ellen was doing the shooting! Charles managed a hearty laugh for the first time since he'd arrived in Paris today. That out of his system, he pounced on Cote for more information.

"You said the third man arrived after the woman fired the gun? What happened then?"

"The third man disarmed the man and the woman and put them on a boat that was waiting," Cote explained.

"A bateau-mouche? Did you see which way it was going? Was there a name on the boat?" Charles asked with a new sense of urgency. "How long ago was this?"

"Oh, I would say it was about an hour ago. The boat was heading in the direction of I'le de la cite. I cannot read, so I can't tell you the name of the boat."

"Thank you, thank you very much my friend." and turning to Bertrand said, "Get the patrol boat down here, vite! And please put this gentleman up in a hotel for tonight." He handed the gypsy a handful of euros and thanked him again profusely."

"I am most grateful, mon amie. You may have saved two lives tonight. Bon chance!"

CHAPTER 59

While Charles was waiting impatiently for the boat to arrive at the quai, we were plotting our next move. I reminded Boutin that Alain and Marco had to have a phone on them. Either it was the phone they'd taken from Boutin or one of their phones, but there was no way in this day and age that neither man possessed a cell phone.

What slowed us down though was how to get it from them without giving either man a chance to escape. Boutin did have a gun now, and that would be an incentive for Marco and

Alain to behave, but there was no telling what the situation in the hold was now. Had they managed to remove their bindings? Were they lying in wait to spring on one of us if we opened the door? Waiting though was just getting us further down the Seine and keeping me away longer from Charles, so we had to do something.

Boutin suggested that I open the door gingerly from a crouch so that if one of our captives were waiting, Boutin could pop over my head with the gun and surprise them. I was ok with that plan but worried that both could be free.

Knowing that we couldn't wait any longer, we took up our positions outside the hold, listening for a moment to determine the state of things inside. We could hear low voices, and the French cursing had stopped, but was that an advantage? At least we knew that if Alain and Marco were still wild enough to yell and swear, it was a good bet that they were still incapacitated. These lower voices could indicate that the men were free and plotting or that they'd tired of trying to free themselves and were quietly discussing soccer. While I knew that Marco couldn't escape the cuffs, I was worried about how well the makeshift bindings on Alain were working. Only one way to find out!

"I'm ready!" I declared with as much enthusiasm as I could muster.

Boutin could see me stiffen as he stood above me and off to the side. I looked up at him for the signal, and when he winked, I rattled the doorknob. Boutin, standing back from the doorway enough to be out of sight, was intensely alert. As the door opened a crack, I could see Marco sitting on a large cardboard box, fully cuffed still. Alain was not in my eyeline, but I knew where he was immediately.

"Ah, our 'captors' have returned. Is torture next?" Alain drawled in the exact arrogant sneering tone that enraged me.

That rage burst out of me, and I hip-checked the door with all of my might in the direction of that irritating voice. I connected, and when I heard the thud and the sound of something sliding slowly to the floor, I knew I had Alain.

Not wasting any time, Boutin rushed past me and found Alain, a former macho military man in a fetal position on the floor, bleeding from a crack over his right eye and a dent in his nose resembling the edge of the door.

I prepared the 'treatment' for Marco -- holding out the rolled-up canvas and advancing toward him with the open champagne bottle perched at a 65-degree angle over it.

"You move, you touch me, I may accidentally spill this bubbly over this precious piece of art. I wonder if the paint will react differently with champagne bubbles than with a non-bubbly liquid? Will it disintegrate the paint faster or no difference? You're an art aficionado, aren't you, Marco? What do you think?" I taunted him.

Marco, his gaze never leaving the juncture of the bottle and the painting, calculated his move. He stood, and began to move forward, which is when I realized that his bindings on his ankles were very loose. "I think it will ruin the painting the same as other liquid. Ruined is ruined. Put the painting down. Hassam didn't paint that so that some ditzy Americaine could ruin it."

"Ok, but he painted it so that you could steal it and deprive the world of his work?" The sarcasm easily matched the tone Marco and Alain had adopted with her. I kept advancing toward to Marco until I was just out of arms reach, and then demanded, with the bottle shaking very slightly,

"Back up -- Vite! Vite! Keep going. My hand is getting very weak" As I continued to advance, he continued moving toward me.

He was almost within reach of the canvas, so I implemented plan B.

"ARRRRRRRRGH!" I growled and simultaneously reached out and clocked Marco with the Champagne bottle while dropping the painting to the floor and kicking it out behind me.

Boutin, having secured Alain with some more wet linens, this time around his ankles, rushed over to help me with Marco. As I doused him with the rest of the Veuve Clicquot, Boutin punched him squarely in the jaw and wrestled him to the ground.

Once Alain and Marco were incapacitated again, Boutin began to search them for a phone. He got lucky on his first try -- Alain, not trusting Marco, had it in the edge of his boot.

"Voila! A phone! What shall we do with this Ellen?" Boutin announced with victorious sarcasm.

Elated and seeing an end to the debacle, I matched his tone perfectly; "Well, Lieutenant, I don't know. Shall we see if we can get a signal, so that our friend Charles and help us deal with this garbage? Do you think he's free?"

Boutin, seeing now what Charles loved about the Americaine -- her spunk and ability to bounce back with amazing wit, laughed for the first time out loud.

Startled by the unfamiliar sound and floating on the edge of a high I'd never experienced before, I joined him in laughing.

Alain and Marco, disheveled, wet, stinking of booze and bleeding could only groan.

CHAPTER 60

Charles paced back and forth on the Quai, waiting impatiently for the patrol boat to arrive. He could hear the engine coming from a distance and was waiting to jump on when it pulled up beside him. He wasted no time in directing the boat - "Allez - a l'est -- they've headed East!"

The boat's driver heard the stress in Blanchard's voice and sped away from the Quai in the direction indicated.

Charles was cursing himself -- he'd seen the bateau-mouche making its way along the Seine and never considered -- even when he knew that the limo had been abandoned by the river -- that Ellen and Boutin could be on it.

I'm not seeing the forest for the trees -- I'm off my game, he mused to himself. Ellen had taken him off his game; something he wasn't sorry about.

After 10 minutes had elapsed, Charles could begin to see the aft of a bateau-mouche, which was moving slowly near the middle of the broadest part of the river. The driver, at Charles' command, throttled down the boat and floated alongside it. To Charles' trained eye, all looked well. There didn't appear to be any sign of anyone on board until he heard the opening of a door and booming laughter.

"We've done it - we're free -- and I can't wait to call Charles! Ellen exulted.

"Mademoiselle, you are the most amazing person I've ever met." Charles smiled at the worshipful tone that Boutin had adopted. Now, he knows how I felt the moment I met her, Charles thought to himself.

Although he'd have liked to eavesdrop a bit more, Charles knew that he had to identify himself and 'rescue' them.

"Ah, so I have scoured Paris all night for you, and here you are -- laughing and joking. "Charles drawled as he lifted himself onto the Bateau.

"Charles!" Stunned, I launched myself at the man that had kept me going since that afternoon in the Musee d'Orsay.

"How did you find us, mon Amie?" Boutin added.

"It's a long story. We'll talk about it later, but for now, where are Marco and Alain?" Charles asked calmly while maintaining a grip on my waist.

"In the hold, drenched in champagne and probably not at all willing to discuss how they were outfoxed by an injured Americaine and an aging flic."

"Oh, and Charles, we have such a surprise for you! Close your eyes and put out your hands." Ellen was ebullient and couldn't resist having a bit of fun with Charles. What they had for him would leave him speechless.

"Really, mon Coeur, can't you just give it to me?" Charles was back to business and was really looking forward to questioning Marco and subjecting Alain to a bit of police harassment.

"Please, Charles -- just do as I ask." Satisfied that the bad guys were under wraps for the moment, Charles complied.

"Which hand?" He asked with a smile he couldn't avoid.

"Both please, and palms up," Ellen demanded in a proud voice.

Charles closed his eyes tightly and held his hands out as directed. Moments later, he felt a weighty piece of canvas touch his waiting hands, and a soft kiss touch his cheek.

"Open them!" Ellen couldn't wait for him to see.

Charles' eyes snapped open and looked down at the object in his hands. "Mon Dieu! Is this what I think it is? How did you manage this?"

Proudly, Boutin announced -- "long story. We'll tell you later."

CHAPTER 61

Hours later, reunited with Cathy and Eleanor, and with the help of my friend Boutin, I told the story of how the Hassam was recovered.

Charles listened intently; amazed at Ellen's instincts and bravery. He should never have doubted her -- or Boutin. His old friend had served him well, and Charles knew he would never forget it. His memories of Isabelle's death haunted him. There'd been nothing he could have done to save her. But Ellen was different; she'd helped to save herself -- along with Boutin's muscle and training.

It was clear from where the Hassam was found, Marco had no intention of returning the Hassam. Without Ellen and Boutin, it most likely would never have been seen again. Now that Marco and Alain had been taken into custody, Charles only had one piece of business left to do—find the Renoir!

CHAPTER 62

After personally tucking Ellen into bed -- a chore Charles realized he wouldn't mind repeating every night -- Charles quietly locked up the suite. Cathy and Eleanor had slipped off to their beds, 1/2 an hour earlier, while Charles was putting Ellen "to bed."

His men were on guard outside, and he wasn't leaving until the morning.

He stretched out on the couch in the sitting room, unable to sleep. He was torn between returning to Ellen and planning his next move. While he was tempted to go in and personally "guard" Ellen from any more danger, he knew in his heart that his responsibility was in restoring the missing painting to the walls of the d' Orsay.

He couldn't help but think back to the 1/2 hour he'd just spent with Ellen; They had lain together on the bed holding each other and whispering. He told her how proud he was of her, and she told him how scared she was. Charles was moved, and he told her that he had been terrified for her but reassured that Boutin was with her to protect her.

After some passionate kissing, Charles knew it was time to withdraw. There'd been enough drama tonight. She was safe, the bad guys in custody and the Hassam under the couch he lay on.

Focusing back on the investigation, Charles knew that the only person he needed to talk to tomorrow was Marco. And he also knew that he wouldn't leave Marco until the Renoir was recovered.

CHAPTER 63

When I awoke, I stayed in bed relishing the time I'd spent last night with Charles. He'd been so loving and caring. We'd laughed softly about my method of recovering the Hassam. And he'd sternly admonished me from getting involved again. And I wouldn't. Charles was no longer in danger--Marco was behind bars as well as the odious Alain -- after a trip to the prison infirmary, I hoped.

Today was my last full day in Paris, and that kind of had me panicked. I knew from Charles himself that he would be interrogating Marco and Alain today until one of them broke.

Charles wanted me to use my last day in Paris to do something fun. Cathy and Eleanor were undoubtedly anxious to get back to their trip, but somehow a journey down the Seine in a bateau-mouche was so 'been there-done that.' Trailing through the Louvre held no further appeal without my personal bodyguard, and I'd already seen the 'big three' -- the Winged Victory of Samothrace and the Venus Di Milo and the Mona Lisa. The one thing we hadn't done -- the one compulsory Paris experience we'd missed was people watching from a cafe. I'll buy a pack of smokes, order a cafe au lait and write in my journal -- something I'd neglected to do over the past several days! I had a lot to add.

Cathy and Eleanor could take the Seine Boat Cruise, and this afternoon, the three of them could go to Montmartre. Satisfied with my plan, I got gingerly out of bed -- trying to ignore my various sore spots.

I walked out to the living room of the suite after a brief visit to the bathroom, to find Cathy and Eleanor sipping coffee and quietly talking.

"Good Morning, my darling!" Cathy said, rising from her seat and giving me a soft hug.

"How are you both today!" I asked, relieved that they'd survived this week with me.

"Much better now that everyone's accounted for" Eleanor chirped - the gusto back in her voice.

I shook my head and halfheartedly chuckled. "How've you enjoyed Paris?"

The three of us laughed, knowing how awful the past several days had been. Now that we were safe and had no guards on us, the sense of relief we felt was palpable.

Cathy poured me a cup of coffee, and we chatted about our week and what we were going to do with our new-found freedom today.

The women liked my idea -- although Cathy was hesitant to leave me on my own.

"I know that you can find trouble in the most unlikely places. I don't know if I'm quite ready to leave you to your own devices."

"I'll be fine. I am going to walk down to the Cafe de la Paix and write in my journal, smoke and drink coffee -- you know? I want to be a Parisian for a day!" I said wistfully.

"Ok -- then Eleanor and I will take the Seine Boat tour -- I've been dying to do it, and I understand your reluctance. So, if you're sure you don't mind?" Cathy too was wistful. Too many of their days in Paris on this trip were caught up with intrigue. Time to enjoy.

CHAPTER 64

It was a beautiful, warm Paris day, and I was excited to embark on my trip to Cafe de la Paix. I dressed casually in the dark linen slacks I'd gotten at the Galeries LaFayette, and along with a sleeveless cream shell and a pale pink scarf knotted at my neck, large black sunglasses, and ballet flats, I realized I looked every inch Parisian. My dark curls had been tamed into submission, and I wore a light pink lipstick. Glancing at myself in the lobby of the St. Jean, I realized that I looked beautiful. I've lost weight, I guess -- must be all that international intrigue, but in my heart - I know what it is -- I've fallen hard for Charles. This was the 'look of love.'

Giggling to myself, and now with that 60's tune stuck in my brain, I continued my walk along the Rue de Rivoli musing to myself that all I've been through this week had agreed with me.

Now there's a diet! International intrigue, danger, injury, fear, fight, and finally, love has given me a glow and a spring that was as unfamiliar as the looks I was getting from the Frenchmen I passed.

When I finally arrived at the Cafe de la Paix, I chose a table at the corner of Boulevard des Capucines and Rue Auber. This way, I could see people approaching from both sides. After ordering my cafe from a very attentive waiter, I took my journal and blue pen from my bag and lit a cigarette.

The cafe was delicious, and I thoroughly enjoyed my seat at the center of things. I got caught up in little intrigues -- the couple obviously fighting (although in French so I couldn't figure out who did what to whom, but by the time the woman poured her coffee in his lap, I had ascertained that the man did her wrong); by the woman sitting alone, tears running down her cheeks as she flipped slowly through a pile of photographs; I wasn't close enough to determine the nature of the pictures, but she was older, and I had a feeling that the photos were of her family.

Finally, there was a darling little girl -- also an American -- who couldn't sit still. She was so excited to be in Paris and kept asking her parents where the princesses were."

After an hour and four cigarettes, I'd absorbed about as much people watching as I could, and I settled down with my journal. So much has happened in the last few days that I found myself quite caught up in remembering and recounting it all. My journal was becoming quite full, but I still hadn't written of Charles. Not that he'd escaped mention, but I found it hard to discuss my feelings and hopes for Charles. Despite our romantic moments, I still found it hard to believe that he felt any way for me at all. It all seems to be a dream - one that there is very little time to wrap up, I realized.

I'm going home tomorrow. I know Charles promised me he'd see me before we left, but he'd made no mention of when and did not try to encourage me to stay.

That worry, above all others, sickened my stomach. *Why wouldn't he ask me to stay if all is well? Perhaps, knowing I had to return to work, he knew I had no option. But why not ask?'*

I knew the answer -- his feelings for me were surface -- temporary. With a sinking heart, I allowed for the fact that I liked him more than he, me. With that depressing thought, I looked up as Eleanor and Cathy approached.

The ladies had enjoyed the cruise – 'a perfect day for it -- sunny and warm!' And we chatted although I had little to add. My cruise had been on a cold dark night, and I spent most of it inside a locked hold.

After a light lunch, Cathy, Eleanor and I set off for Montmartre.

CHAPTER 65

Charles knew he had quite a task ahead of him. His prisoner -- Marco was well known to him. And, he was also his cousin, although that familial relationship was little in evidence now. At one time, he and Marco had been very close -- like brothers almost. But something changed the summer Charles' father died. He supposed that it was as hard on Marco (he'd been known as Marc then) as it had been on himself.

Charles Blanchard the 1st was a surrogate father to Marc. His own father Mathias

Duclos had died tragically in an automobile accident when Marc was 6. Since that time, Charles' father had taken him under his wing. Marc had always felt he was a second-class relation, and Charles the 1st wanted him to feel as if he belonged. He'd loved his sister's husband like a brother and worried about how she'd raise Marc alone. So, he set about including him in all the family memories. They spent many long hours together poring over the family treasures, visiting museums as Charles' father tried to impress his pedigree on him. Charles himself had participated in these trips and reminiscences but was more confident in his place in the family.

When Charles' father died, Charles took it very hard. But he'd been 18 then and preparing for University. Marc, 4 years younger, lost both Charles and his father that summer. He began hanging out with other boys on the Mont who were not likely to further their academics.

Marc's mother died when he was 16, and that seemed to have been the turning point for him. He began to complain about being the 'poor relation' because he was brought to live with Charles' family. At 18 he was asked to leave home because he'd become belligerent and had started stashing family heirlooms in hiding places around Mont St. Michel.

Charles -- graduate of a justice program discovered what he'd been doing and at first, tried to reason with him.

"These things belong to you, but cousin, they also belong to the rest of us. If you wanted something, you should have discussed it with us."

Marc replied angrily, "I know what I'm entitled to! I am a son of the Blanchards -- even though I'm an orphan! I shouldn't have to ask!"

He and Marc had argued many times about this until the relationship became so strained that they no longer tried.

Charles lit a cigarette and mused, *and that's when he began to bait me with ever-escalating crimes. Not just crimes against the family -- but larger more public heists. It stops today.* He threw his cigarette impatiently on the ground and turned on his heel, heading back inside to his face-off with Marc/Marco.

CHAPTER 66

Montmartre was a beehive of activity. Since there were only 3 of us left in our group, we took a taxi to the top of the hill and worked our way down. Sacré Coeur was magnificent, and Montmartre didn't disappoint - from the 5-star view of Paris spread below, to the soaring spires and ancient wooden doors.

We paused from time to time to eavesdrop on tours -- getting enough information to satisfy us and then we moved on.

Cathy stood below the stairs at the scenic overlook and looking back at the church, proclaimed in a small voice -- "It's like we're approaching Heaven. Doesn't it seem that way? Up here in the clouds -- Paris below -- God above."

I didn't know my Aunt to be so sentimental and schmaltzy before, but I felt it too.

"Cathy, if this is Heaven, I'm in the right place!" I squeezed her shoulders.

We poked around the village of Montmartre, peering over artist's shoulders as they worked and declining invitations to be drawn by them.

But, as I stood back for a moment and watched Cathy and Eleanor laughing at a fresh Frenchman, I realized I wanted to preserve this moment forever.

"Msr. - would you draw the three of us together?" I asked the Frenchman.

"Ah -- Bon! It will be my masterpiece. Not un belle mademoiselle - but trois! An offer I can't refuse."

I pulled Eleanor and Cathy over to me, and we fussed for a few moments about how best to pose. But in the end, Eleanor and Cathy threw their arms around me, and Eleanor declared - "the best pose of all -- the three of us together, alive and out of trouble!"

"Thank you, Charles!" The three of us shouted together.

Cathy and I laughed along with Eleanor and the artist, chuckling, began to draw.

The end product was indeed a masterpiece. He captured the sparkling eyes of Cathy and Eleanor and the happy, yet winsome look in mine. When he finished, the artist, who was named René, presented it to us, and we were delighted with the result.

Cathy was drawn to perfection--blonde, poised and dignified; her blue eyes and red lips bright and happy. Eleanor too looked lovely; her short grey hair, slightly rumpled by the breeze, a broad smile spread across her cheekbones. Looking very aristocratic.

I was surprised to see myself as the artist did. *Boy -- he really cleaned me up*, I thought.

Where were my pudgy cheeks? That sparkle in my brown eyes seemed to light up the page, and my hair was practically drawn as a halo. And for the second time that day, I felt pretty.

Parting with 50 euros for the drawing was no problem for me. I'd easily have paid 10 times as much.

We bid adieu to René - a la Francais -- a kiss on each cheek from each of us, and effusive praise for his talents.

Buoyed by that experience -- I hadn't expected to enjoy it -- we moseyed around the village square, in and out of small shops. After an hour or more we found a tiny tea room on the street opposite Le Moulin de la Galette - a fabulous mill, and windmill featured, ironically, in the painting Charles sought - stolen the other night from the D'Orsay!

Noticing the time, Cathy suggested we find a taxi and head back to the hotel. We had packing to do and wanted a nap before our last night in Paris.

CHAPTER 67

Charles interrogation of Marco was going nowhere. Charles had played the family card and the hard-ass cop card, and neither worked. It was, as if, on that long-ago day when Marc left the family home on Mont St, Michel, he had died and Marco had risen in his place. A Marco with no sense of family; no sense of right or wrong; no sense of self-preservation.

He was not belligerent or sarcastic. Just silent. Charles tried to work out if the silence had to do with his embarrassment at being caught or his determination to see Charles ruined.

"Marc--Marco! I am trying to understand why you'd steal the Hassam, which already belongs to you as part of our heritage -- and then let it come back to me so easily. You and Alain could easily have taken Ellen and Boutin. Boutin may have given you trouble, but he was concerned with protecting Ellen. I'm sure you realized that which leads me to believe that it was your graceless way of getting the Hassam back into my hands.

"And," Charles drew a long breath here and lit a cigarette while turning away from his cousin.

"And so, that leads me to believe that what you were really after was the Renoir. Something that belongs to neither of us, but to the French people."

Marco continued his campaign of silence. Although Charles noticed that his eyes had twitched when he realized that Charles was on to him. Marco had been paid very well for the Renoir and needed the money. He had set a lot aside over the years as a result of his illegal occupation. But now he wanted to retire. There was a woman in the South of France who was waiting for him to come home -- to her and to his boy. But now his cousin had him locked up and it looked like that long lazy retirement was not going happen. Sylvie had been his lover and his life for fifteen years -- and just six years ago, she bore him a son. Gaspard was a lively little boy who idolized his father. Marc wanted to be as good a father to him as Charles' father had been to Marc.

He could feel himself un-tensing and letting go of something he had held onto for so many years - his resentment of Charles. He sensed that Charles was looking for a way to rescue the Renoir with as few complications as possible. And for Marc, he now wanted more than ever before to start a new path. The problem was his buyer. He had paid dearly for something that was now in Marc's power to deliver or withhold.

CHAPTER 68

I paced up and down in front of the hotel. Several days ago, I wouldn't have attempted such a dangerous maneuver, but now with Alain and Marco in stir, I felt safe again. And surely if Charles wanted me out front on my own, he believed it was safe as well.

I wondered what was keeping Charles. He'd rung a few hours ago and asked me to be waiting outside for him. We were going to dinner on our own. Eleanor and Cathy were dining in the Ritz restaurant that evening.

I was thrilled that Charles wanted to see me alone and was hoping that he'd want to talk of our future.

Just at that moment, a car drew to the curb, and Paris' hottest flic emerged.

"Cherie!" Sorry, I'm late, but I've been trying to break Marco since early this morning. And we've had a breakthrough. And for that, I also am very sorry, because it means I must leave you. I have to follow a very time-sensitive lead."

"Charles -- do you mean you're standing me up on my last night in Paris? Can't Boutin or someone else follows that lead?" Tears pricked at my eyes. Seeing him tense, I knew he was feeling torn. What was it about their timing that never allowed for their romance to blossom?

"Ellen, I really am sorry -- you must know I'd rather be with you. But I know I'll see you again and I've promised myself that. This tip can't wait. If the Renoir gets into the wrong hands, we will surely never see it again. It is my responsibility to France to see that that doesn't happen." Charles knew he was on thin ice, but he couldn't trust the conclusion of this case to anyone else. His blood was involved.

"How long will you be gone? Our flight isn't until Mid-day tomorrow. Perhaps we'll catch a few moments together." I suggested, suddenly hopeful.

Charles turned back towards the car and with haste tinged with regret, spoke. "Cher Ellen, I cannot guarantee you anything -- what I know now is that I am very close to recovering the Renoir and I must pursue this lead. I'm very sorry, but this is MY job and MY responsibility. I will find you when this is cleared up, but I cannot tell you if that would be today, tomorrow or a month from now. Charles rushed back toward Ellen, his heart aching as he saw the hurt on her face.

"My darling, go home, and I will come to you when the Renoir once again hangs on the walls of the d'Orsay." With that, he planted a passionate kiss on my mouth and was gone.

CHAPTER 69

DeGaulle was a horror show when we arrived. Lines snaked down the main corridor. Cathy and Eleanor now showing their exhaustion from the trip had checked their luggage at the curb and were in the process of winding their way along to the front of the check-in line. I'd come along a bit behind them after paying the taxi driver and issuing a few instructions to the men on the curb. Risking a French smack-down by cutting in line, I came quietly up alongside them.

I could see their lined faces and the subtle slouch of their shoulders. I forgot that these two women had been through a harrowing experience of their own -- the kidnapping, gassing, and detainment in the hotel basement. And while the last few days they appeared okay, it must have been adrenaline that kept them going.

For a moment, I felt guilty for giving them another moment's stress, but I had no choice. And so, I talked quietly with them and made them see the sense in my plan.

CHAPTER 70

I Didn't get on the plane.

I did, however, get back into my taxi and return to Paris.

Eleanor and Cathy were surprised at my plan -- and Cathy, ever the pragmatist, inquired what I would do with my luggage.

I turned to her with an embarrassed look and said, "Cathy -- my luggage is still at the hotel. I'm sorry I lied to you and told you I took it down early to the cab, but I was afraid you would argue with me about staying, and I have to stay. You understand, don't you?"

"Honey -- of course I understand -- you're in love with Charles, and you don't want to go home. But there is nothing you can do right now -- he is off pursuing a lead, and you don't know where. I'm worried you'll be in danger again and he won't be here to help you."

"Well, I promise you I won't interfere with the investigation, but I want to be there when it ends. I have to be. Our story started with me, and it will end with me. I have plans for Charles and me, and I know that despite Charles' distraction right now, he has plans for us. I'm not willing to wait for him to find me at home. I'm going to find him."

"I promise I'll be safe."

And I was -- I had the taxi stop on the Rue de Rivoli, and I purchased a cell phone.

The waiting taxi took me back to the Ritz, and once in the protection of my room, I made a phone call.

CHAPTER 71

Charles was up to his neck in fish -- and not the nice buttery fish he'd have indulged in at his favorite restaurant -- but smelly, uncooked fish - recently offloaded from a boat in Calais.

The hot tip he had was also a significant risk. Marco had convinced him that he should continue with the meeting he'd scheduled with his buyer. The exchange of payment was to take place on a fishing boat at Calais Harbor. The British buyer was rumored to have heavy political influence in France, England, and America.

Malcolm Lattimore, the man who had contracted Marco to steal the Renoir, was well known in the art world as a prodigious collector of Impressionist and Romantic works. Many rumors have circulated over the decades of dirty deals done by Lattimore -- including the use of blackmail to obtain objects of his desire. Never proven though, was the rumor of a vast collection made possible by theft and underground machinations.

Charles had looked at Lattimore during investigations in the past, but he was never able to prove his involvement. There was the heist of the Degas from a private collection, a Monet stolen from the artist's own studio in Giverney and the stunning theft of a Lautrec canvas also from a private French collection last year. Each case remained unsolved, although -- truth be told, Charles had not investigated those cases himself. In each case, the paintings had entirely disappeared from view -- never to be seen again.

It was that fear -- that Lattimore would get away with treasure again, that convinced Charles to trust Marco -- just once.

Marco had convinced him that he wanted to return to the fold. Wanted to have sweet life with Sylvie and his son. He had too much to risk by screwing Charles. Charles hoped he meant it.

And, because he wanted to give his cousin that chance. Charles was closing out this investigation on his own. He'd shut Boutin out by telling him that Marco was an informant and would only deal with Charles alone.

From his perch behind a tub of shrimp, Charles saw a man in aviator glasses approach Marco. The two men shook hands, and Marco followed him towards a vessel tied up in the harbor.

Charles counted to 30 and followed the two men. As he approached the vessel, he'd seen them heading for, Charles noticed Marco's companion throw off the bowline and push off from the dock.

He was prepared for this and approached the yacht and captain he'd hired earlier that afternoon.

Charles followed the boat from a distance until it approached the shipping lanes, where it stopped just short of the shipping channel. His captain was loath to continue further because it was growing dark and he worried about commercial vessels swamping their boat. A few hundred Euros quenched his concern, and as darkness began to fall, Charles convinced him to power down the motor and hoist the sails -- he wanted his approach to be as silent as possible. The fishing vessel had remained at anchor, which,

Charles thought was very considerate of them.

After an hour of drifting, Charles was just feet from the vessel, when he heard a gunshot, followed moments later by the sound of the anchor being raised and the motor starting. Charles was fortunate to be close enough -- just -- and he hoisted himself aboard. His captain was only too happy to head home.

CHAPTER 72

Back at the Ritz, I settled in for a wait.

My new cellphone sat beside me – quiet for the moment. I had kept my promise to Aunt Cathy – I was not going to get myself involved in the investigation again. I wanted Charles to finish it up and come home safely. That being said, I also wanted to know what was going on – so last night I contacted a new friend who it turns out was available to help me out.

The fact that my new friend was the second conquest I'd made of a French man – and cop, still had me stunned, but after that night on the Seine, Boutin was solidly in my corner. I didn't flatter myself that he was in love with me – as I hoped Charles was – after all Boutin had a pretty wife and small daughter at home (information I'd gotten from him as we were tied up in the limo and bateau-mouche two nights before). But, Boutin was enthralled by me – he told me so, after the Great Champagne Attack.

Boutin told me that he'd never met anyone with less training but better instincts in all the time in the Suretè. My naiveté of all things law enforcement had worked in my favor. I'm sure that I just had more imagination. And I liked my new nickname.

Just at that moment my cellphone rang – it's ringtone, suitably the Marsellaise – and I answered the phone to that greeting;

"Bonjour M'selle MacGyver – I am calling in to report. Charles just boarded a yacht in Calais Harbor. He's following a boat, which Marco boarded with another man. Fortunately for me – I was prepared. The boat hired by Charles is being driven by the brother of a man I know 'ere. He let me know, and I have hired him to follow Charles and the boat Marco is on."

"Charles did not want me involved, clearly to protect Marco – and I cannot blame him. Marco is making good here. He's 'returned' the Hassam and has promised to return the Renoir. Fortunately, and I hope my good friend Charles appreciates this, I shall be here to assist, should trouble arise." Boutin was in good humor. He liked the idea of 'being there for Charles,' and he loved the effect that Ellen had on Charles.

"Jean Boutin you are a good man and a better friend! I know Charles will be grateful for your help, whatever is needed. Call me if things should change."

CHAPTER 73

Jean Boutin smiled to himself as he hung up the phone. He did indeed like Ellen, and he was happy to have his friend Charles involved with another woman. He, like Georges, had known Charles for many years and he too had seen the change in Charles after his first wife was killed. This man with Ellen was a new man.

He continued his surveillance of the boat convoy he'd become part of. As night fell, he knew that Charles would take the chance to board the still fishing vessel, but he was concerned that there may be others on the boat besides Lattimore and Marco. Boutin stood ready to jump into action.

10 minutes later, he did just that in response to the same gunshot that had urged Charles aboard.

Charles had entered on the Portside and Boutin, Starboard. Both men, unaware of the other crept quietly along the deck their ears tuned for signs of a struggle. The boat was quiet, but all of a sudden reversed direction and headed back to the harbor. Boutin was thrown off balance by the sudden movement and crashed into the rail. He tried to quiet his grunt, but the severe jarring he took felt as if it had cracked a rib. The noise was enough to alert Charles, who approached him gun drawn, breaking into a smile when he saw who it was.

Charles helped Boutin to his feet and without a word, the two men proceeded down into the hull on cats' feet.

What they saw on entrance was a beaming Marco at the wheel, the rolled-up Renoir propped against the wall of the ship and an angry Lattimore, bleeding from his thigh - which Marco had put a tourniquet around – after handcuffing him to a steam pipe.

"Ready to go home, Cousin?" Marco remarked cheerily.

"Oui -- I'm ready," Charles replied with pride.

CHAPTER 74

Boutin allowed Charles to question his cousin privately. He knew that there were things to be said and revealed which Boutin had no right to know. And, Boutin had a phone call to make.

"Oui -- 'allo? M'selle McGyver? C'est Fini. We are heading back to Calais. We should be in Paris by 4 am. Shall I continue as directed by your plan?"

"Sil vous plait - Jean -- I will meet you at six. Merci."

CHAPTER 75

Things moved swiftly after they returned to shore. Charles had a car waiting to return to Paris. Lattimore was settled quickly into it after a quick check by medical personnel. Marco 'drifted' away at some point, and neither Charles nor Boutin seemed curious about where he'd gone.

Charles had debriefed Marco on the boat and knew that he'd retrieved the painting from its hiding place in Montmartre, prior to heading for Calais -- Charles had actually followed him there.

Once on the boat, Marco told him Lattimore was suspicious of the yacht on the harbor -- Charles' boat -- and had deliberately anchored to determine if they were being followed.

Marco had tried his best to deny any knowledge of who would be following them, but Lattimore knew better and had drawn a gun. Marco -- knowing that Lattimore was older and considerably less in shape than he, had managed to wrestle the gun from him and in the ensuing scuffle, the gun had fired, and Lattimore was injured.

Charles was enormously grateful and proud of Marco -- for his integrity and for his compassion in seeing that Lattimore's wound was treated.

In the car now and 1/2 hour from Paris, Charles withdrew from his reverie and thanked Boutin for his assistance and care.

"My friend -- I was never so glad as I was to see you on the deck of that boat. I was afraid that the situation was reversed, and that Marco was the one injured -- and I was expecting Lattimore to surprise me with a bullet. And," he paused here. "And, that bastard of a boat driver took off before I could retrieve my gun -- I was unarmed!" The friends shared a hearty laugh with Lattimore grimacing in pain and frustration.

An hour later, Lattimore was booked and in his cell. Charles looked at the clock and realized that it was 4 in the morning, and he still had work to do. As tired as he was, though, he didn't mind, because he was going to be on a plane to America later in the morning and he could sleep then.

CHAPTER 76

At 5:45, Charles looked up, bleary-eyed as he finished his last report. The Renoir had been retrieved very eagerly by the curator of the D'Orsay, who didn't at all mind coming out in the middle of the night. The Hassan had been returned to the Louvre yesterday morning. All was well. And, he looked forward to 3 hours from now when he boarded his flight to the US and to Ellen.

"Amie? Time to go -- I'll take you home." Boutin offered, having approached him silently from behind."

"Non, Jean -- go home to your wife. I will catch a taxi."

"Charles, I go right by your house. Let me take you home."

"Oui. Merci."

Dawn was beginning to break as they came out onto the street. The street lights were beginning to fade, but darkness still hovered over the city. It was going to be a beautiful dawn though, Charles thought. Pink was beginning to light the horizon - from darkest to lightest.

Charles paid little attention during the brief drive, but when the car stopped by the Quai du Louvre at the Pont des Arts, he asked Boutin what was going on.

"One more loose-end to tie up, mon amie. Down on the Quai." Boutin said mysteriously. Charles looked confused, but he trusted this man and knew Boutin meant well.

Charles quickly descended the steps down to the Quai and began to hear quiet music -- and looking confused he turned around. What he saw brought a smile to his lips.

Standing in the shadows, beautifully dressed in the gown he'd bought her, stood Ellen.

She approached him tentatively as he approached her. When they were a breath apart, Ellen said in her most quiet of voices, "Shall we dance?"

THE END

ABOUT THE AUTHOR

I am Meg McNamara, novelist, Francophile, and adopted mom to a golden retriever named Lucy. My day job is for an arts organization, where inspiration is a daily perk.

I am also CeCe deLuc, romantic writer and author of Love Aix, recently released romantic fiction, set in Aix-en-Provence.

My Dad, also a writer, mentioned in one of his newspaper columns that I had written a story about the theft of the Crown Jewels when I was 7 or 8 years old.

Dad was amused enough about my penchant for drama to quote me in that column. 'The Queen was so mad you could fry an egg on her!', was my first re-tweet -- if you will.

Well, Dad knew something about me that day more than 40+ years ago, and that was that I am a writer -- and a daydreamer.

I am also the author of "Little Noelle's Christmas Wish", a book for children imagining the Eiffel Tower as the world's biggest Christmas Tree.

www.ingramcontent.com/pod-product-compliance
Lightning Source LLC
Chambersburg PA
CBHW051528100726
47898CB00005B/1615